WHITE CROW

WHITE CROW

Marcus Sedgwick

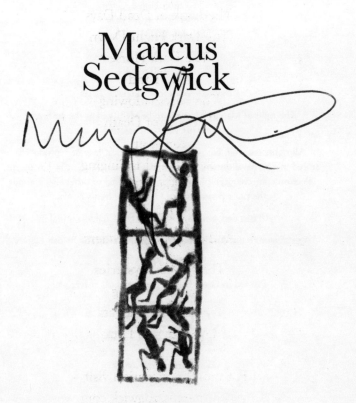

Orion
Children's Books

First published in Great Britain in 2010
by Orion Children's Books
a division of the Orion Publishing Group Ltd
Orion House
5 Upper St Martin's Lane
London WC2H 9EA
An Hachette UK company

3 5 7 9 10 8 6 4 2

All text decorations inspired by the Chaldon mural

A catalogue record for this book is available from the British Library.

ISBN 978 1 84255 187 5

Printed in Great Britain by Clays Ltd, St Ives plc

www.orionbooks.co.uk

For Fiona

Resurrection

The earth quakes, the graves burst open, the dead arise
and stream on in endless procession. The trumpets of the
apocalypse ring out.

There is no judgment,
    no sinners,
    no just men,
    no great
    and no small;
    there is no punishment
    and no reward.
    A feeling of overwhelming love fills us with bliss.

We know, and are.
    And we know with all certainty.
    God *does* exist.

Rebecca

She could have been anyone.

She could have been any girl who arrived in Winterfold that summer.

That sounds strange, doesn't it?

It sounds strange to my ears, anyway. Summer in Winterfold. How can there ever be any other season here but winter, with a name like that? But whatever the time of year, Winterfold has a cold embrace, and like the snows of winter, it does not let you go easily.

Once upon a time there was a whole town here, not just a handful of houses. A town with twelve churches and thousands of people, dozens of streets, and a busy harbour.

And then the sea ate it.

Storm by storm, year by year, the cliffs collapsed into the advancing sea, taking the town with it, house by house and street by street, until all that was left was a triangle of three streets, a dozen houses, an inn, a church. Well, most of it . . .

And then, that summer, she arrived. And actually I'm lying.

She couldn't have been anyone, because the moment I

saw her beautiful face I knew I loved her, and I knew she would love me too.

I knew.

Rebecca slides out of her father's car and the first thing she notices is the smell.

She sniffs the air, and without knowing it, she tries to break it all down. She gets some of it. She gets the hot salty air of the seaside, the tar of the fishing boats hauled up on the beach just out of sight over the ridge, the marram grass of the marshes inland, the hot engine oil because her father has flogged the old car all the way from Greenwich to this God-forgotten place.

She pulls back a long curl of hair blown into her face by the stiff breeze from the shore. Her father pops the boot on the car and grabs both of her bags at once.

The tiny cottage, idiotically named The Mansion, is disappointing; dark, with low ceilings.

Her father drops the bags on a shabby rug, kicks the door shut behind him with the heel of his boot.

'Well,' he says, but Rebecca already doesn't want to hear. She knows what's coming next. 'Your home for the next six weeks. Welcome.'

He's trying to sound carefree, and opens his arms as if

5

he thinks she'll run into them.

She doesn't. Slowly his arms fall back to his sides.

'Your room's at the top of the stairs. Here, I'll show you.'

'I'll find it,' Rebecca says, taking her bags. She turns her back on him, though even as she does so she hates herself.

Her room is a little better than downstairs. She drops her stuff and goes to the window, pulling her backpack off as she does and throwing it on the bed.

There is the sea.

Just beyond the ridge that slopes up to the right to become the cliffs, there's the beach, and the sea, and it burns brightly blue this afternoon, a diamond sea sparkling in the hot sun.

She turns to her backpack on the bed, knowing she has lost.

For a moment she wonders what exactly it is that she's lost, and decides it's a few different things, though what she feels most is that she's lost the battle to stop hurting herself.

The bag had been between her feet all the way from Greenwich, and yes, they'd had the radio on loud to hide the fact that neither of them was speaking, but even so, she would have heard it.

So she knows that Adam hasn't rung, and she knows

there's no point looking, but unable to stop herself she unzips the front pocket, and pulls out her phone.

She stares at the blank screen. Nothing. Nothing. No texts. No missed calls.

For a second she tells herself there's probably been no reception since halfway through the journey, but she has a couple of bars.

So she knows that he's not interested. She tells herself to be strong, but that lasts for five short heartbeats, and then she pushes redial.

When he answers he sounds surprised to hear her.

'Becky?'

She hasn't thought what she's going to say, so it comes out, blunt and raw.

'You said you'd call.'

'I did.'

'No you didn't. You said you'd call. Three days ago.'

'I will,' he lies, barely trying to sound as though he means it.

'You won't, because I left today,' Rebecca stabs, 'So you won't be coming round now. You . . .'

'Becky, listen . . . You don't need to . . . Look, I've got to go.'

Then there's laughter at the other end of the phone. Several voices. His mates. A girl's high-pitched laughter rises over the babble.

Rebecca holds the phone away from her head as if

it's burning her. Slowly, she moves her thumb over the keys and ends the call. She drops the phone on the bed and stares at it for a long minute, then goes downstairs, fingering the silver crucifix Adam gave her for her birthday. It wasn't a religious thing. More a Goth thing.

Until then, she'd always worn a silver heart pendant. It had been given to her by her dad, years ago, when Mum had died. He'd told Rebecca it was so she'd always remember he was there for her, that he loved her, even when they weren't together. But when Adam gave her the crucifix, she'd taken off the heart pendant, and not worn it since.

Maybe her dad had noticed. Neither of them had said anything about it. She tried not to feel bad about it; she wasn't Daddy's little girl any more, it was stupid to cling to that kind of stuff anyway.

Her father comes out of the kitchen.

'Nice room, isn't it?'

She opens the front door.

'I'm going out,' she says.

'I'll do something quick. For seven. Don't be too long.'

But she's already gone, into the hot late afternoon, and she's so preoccupied that she's unaware of the various eyes that are appraising her.

The new girl.

She blinks in the blazing sun, and looks to her left and right. She turns left, and passes the pub. Briefly she notices the sign. The Angel. It's beautiful, handmade, maybe years old, but someone has freshly repainted it. A beautiful stylised angel, handsome, with blond curling hair and glowing white robes, a golden halo and a golden sword. He stares into the blue-sky corner of the sign, as if staring up to God. His face is serene, and yet full of yearning too.

The inn marks the end of the street, and here the road turns back inland, up past the ruins of the priory, so she takes the track down to the beach, but has only taken a few steps when she sees a footpath leading into the darkness of the woods on the cliff.

The beach is full of happy laughing people, sunshine and sea, and joy. All these things feel dead to her. She considers the path up into the darkness, where she can take her pain away from all the brightness, and hide it.

That's the way she chooses.

1798, 7m, 13d.

There came a newcomer to Winterfold today, and God-
to-tell, that is a rare enough happening, but further to
that, something even more remarkable. He has taken the
Hall.

At the inn, they say he is French, and his name is
indeed French. He is called Dr Barrieux, but Martha told
me that his voice is not foreign, but that he speaks English
as Jesus did.

Bless Martha. At least she cooks passably well.

1798, 7m, 27ð.

I learned more of our newcomer today, and yes, Grimes at the Angel Inn said to me that indeed he is newly come from France, from Paris. From Paris! To Winterfold! Think on that. From that most recent hotbed of foment and revolution to our sleepy village, a backwater on any map.

He has taken the Hall, Winterfold Hall, even though it has been empty these long years. For sure, Grimes says, he has been placing a great number of orders for supplies, for vittles and drink, for tools and diverse materials, and also various items of function not known to Grimes.

1798, 8m, 4d.

A hot day today, and one on which wearing the cloth of God was a great burden. I sweltered through my duties, and of course gave succour to the needy and comfort to the weak, but God curse me, I was only too ready to return to the rectory and divest myself at the end of the day.

I lay on my cot, naked like a baby, listening to the seas on the shore, hoping to feel the coolness of the coast stroke my fat belly, but there was not a breath of breeze. It was as hot as Hell.

As Hell.

If Hell is indeed hot.

Bring Me To Life

I might have been normal but if I was I cannot remember that time.

Once, for my birthday, my mother gave me a book of poetry. It was a book of poems that she had written, because she was a poet, and she had written a whole cycle of poems about me. The first ones she had written before I was born, when she was pregnant with me, and the others when I was small.

'This is your gift,' she said to me. 'Your gift from me. It's better than chocolate, or a toy, because no one else has these poems, and they will last forever.'

I was eight years old.

I remember that I nodded solemnly.

'Mother,' I said, 'you are a genius; you are a poet just like Shakespeare. Like him, you have suns, planets, ants, frightening skeletons. I prefer things which are frightening.'

I was eight years old when I said that.

Mother smiled but even as she did I could see sadder things in her eyes behind her smile.

The weekend drags by for Rebecca as she realises just how little there is to do in Winterfold. Her father, though he has nothing to do, spends the time finding ways of being busy, of being away, of being absent. He goes for long walks, presumably to try and clear his head.

She hardly sees him.

She lies on her bed for hour after hour, killing three books from cover to cover and as she ends each one drops them broken-spined onto the rough old floorboards.

They collide briefly during mealtimes, until on Tuesday her father's early return to the house forces her out into the heat.

She explores Winterfold. It takes about twenty minutes. She tells herself off for being a silly city girl, and explores it again properly. This time it takes twenty-five.

There's The Street, where their rented cottage is. It nestles halfway along the row, with its back to the sea, a late medieval cottage with two and a half rooms down and two rooms up. No two houses are alike; there are some older cottages, some more recent ones, probably Victorian. It's like a short lesson in the architecture of English villages. The Street runs parallel to the shore, but the sea is almost entirely hidden behind the houses.

At its northern end is the village shop and a junction. A road leads across the marshes to Crowburgh, while The Street dog-legs sharply back inland, with one or two expensive old houses dotted down either side. She can hear a garden party in full swing behind a high brick wall, the raucous music at odds with the Englishness of it all.

She turns and walks back along The Street, past The Mansion.

At the southern end is the pub, from where a small unmade road bumbles down to the beach car park, where a notice warns that it can get flooded at times of exceptional tide. The sign brings a smile to her face: a solemn diagram of a car half under water, a stick-man driver standing on its roof waving for help.

Here the road turns back sharply inland, running past the entrance to the ruins of the Priory, once thriving, now just ghosts and stones. Further on are more big houses behind high walls and hedges, until this road meets the one coming from the other end of The Street, and the triangle that is Winterfold is completed.

Rebecca finds herself at the entrance to the path into

the woods again, and again she is drawn in.

She notices another, easier path, straighter, running along the back of the woods, but it looks well used, the sort of path dog walkers take to make sure they have a chat with someone. So she chooses the smaller, steeply twisting path into the thin sliver of woods that stands between her and the sea.

She waits a moment as her eyes adjust to the gloom after the bright sunshine of the village, enjoying the sudden cool of the greenness. She retraces her steps from Saturday, but sees a glimpse of blue through the thick undergrowth, and impulsively she pushes off the track and through elder bushes and nettles.

She finds herself in a new universe, just a few paces wide.

What she has found is a clearing in the woods, once probably well inland, but now eaten in half by the cliffs. Behind her, she's hemmed in by a semicircle of densely packed branches and leaves, a wall. She stands on a patch of neatly cropped grass, right up to the point where the land falls away, and beyond that is the infinity of the sea.

It's like a little room, without a roof, and with natural walls and floor, and the best view of the sea anyone could have. There ought to be a bench, but there isn't, and somehow that pleases her. She wonders who keeps the grass short, then notices the rabbit droppings everywhere.

17

The temptation to jump comes on her suddenly.

There is the cliff in front of her, only steps away, and timidly, like a frightened cat, she creeps towards the drop.

She's very close to the edge before she sees just how high the cliff is. She can see the beach below, and she knows it would be enough to kill her if she fell.

She pictures herself stepping off, and it makes her head swim, so she creeps back and gazes out at the sea.

It's a unique place, and though she can hear sounds from the village over the rush of the waves on the beach, it feels a million miles from anywhere or anyone.

It's the need for the comfort of childhood that starts her daydreaming. It's a safe thing to do, something which does not rely on her father, or Adam, or anyone else. Happy memories are invincible, protected and protecting, no one can destroy them.

Words drift into her head, images from books. For some reason she's thinking of Treasure Island, but she knows why; she's found the best pirate's look-out point that ever was. Treasure Island, Robinson Crusoe, Swiss Family Robinson. Then music. She's thinking about the cliffs and a song about bluebirds, but not even realising she's got two different songs mixed up, the song in her head is Dorothy's from The Wizard of Oz.

She remembers the production at little school, smiling, remembering the blue gingham dress that she wore, and wonders if she can still hit those first two notes, a whole octave apart.

'Some-where.'

She falters, stops, and tries again, louder this time, and hits it perfectly.

'Some – Where.'

And before she can utter another note, the line is finished by a voice behind her.

'Over the rainbow, bluebirds fly . . .'

Her heart racing, Rebecca spins round, catching her heel on a rabbit hole.

She falls, and knowing the cliff is at her back, her hands flail wildly, grasping for the ground.

She ends up on her side, winded, her head hanging into thin clear space.

She looks up into the eyes of the strangest-looking girl she's ever seen.

The strange girl says a strange word.

'Ferelith.'

Rebecca faints.

Four Sea Interludes – I

I left school when I was fourteen.

I left because there was nothing else that anyone could teach me. I know this sounds like I'm boasting, but it's just the truth. It was on the day that I found myself explaining Game Theory to my maths teacher that I knew there was no point being there any longer.

I got up from my seat, ignoring all the names and the insults from the others.

'Ferelith!' my teacher yelled. 'Sit down!'

I didn't.

I walked out of the classroom, straight out of the school gates, and down to the bypass, and I put my thumb out until a truck stopped and I hitch-hiked all the way home.

When I got home I expected a lecture about how dangerous it was to hitch-hike, but my father had other things on his mind.

That was the day I realised that if there is a God in the sky then he's vindictive and cruel, because I arrived home to find my mother being taken away in an ambulance. There actually were men in white coats. It's really funny if you think about it.

But I tried not to.

I visited Mother a few weeks later, but the trip to the home that she had been sent to upset me so much that my father never took me again. Anyway, he lost interest after a couple of months, not just in her but in me too, so that was that and when he went away I was left on my own.

So instead I made Winterfold my own, my own place, and I continued my education, in two ways. First, I used the internet, because I couldn't afford the bus into town to go to the library, and anyway the library is really old and the books on the shelves there are dying.

Secondly, I continued my education in a more important way, through the observation of everyone around me, because nothing is more important to learn in life than the interaction of a human being with another human being.

And that's what I did for a few years, and it suited me fine. Winterfold was the perfect place for my strange life. Claustrophobic. I lived a life of confinement while I bided my time. Maybe it's not how everyone lives, but I don't mind about that.

I think I was waiting, though I didn't know what I was waiting for. I think, though, that I knew I was waiting not for something, but for someone.

So when I heard there was a new girl in the village, I went to find her and I found her in the Lover's Seat.

I watched her for a few moments, and decided she was as beautiful as they'd said in the pub. She had her back to

21

me, so I hadn't seen her face yet, just her winding red hair. I tried to think of what colour it was; burnt caramel, sunset corn, honey beer, and then I thought I sounded like the dumb names they give paint in the big DIY place in town. So I stopped that.

She was singing! From my favourite film. I only needed two notes to recognise it, and so I joined in, but I think I scared her, which was stupid of me.

She turned as she fell, and I rushed to her.

I leaned over her and I think she must have thought that she'd fallen right over the cliff, because her eyes rolled back in her head and closed.

I couldn't pick her up, but I managed to pull her back away from the edge, and then I sat with her, as she lay on the grass.

I didn't look at her straightaway, I'm not sure why. Maybe she was too beautiful, too dazzling? No, that's dumb. Maybe I just wanted to draw it out, discovering her face, I mean. So I looked and saw the softness of her skin, which as far as I could see was utterly perfect.

That was enough for now, and so I sat with her till she woke up, my hand resting on her hair as she breathed lightly, watching the sunlight on the sea.

1798, 8m, 19ð.

For the space of nigh a whole fourteen-night the Lord saw fit to visit upon me a sore and tiresome succession of bodily evils, which kept me abed until yesterday around Vesper.

Today being the Lord's day, I performed my duties, now, God-to-praise, mercifully freed of my sicknesses. I confess that even as I performed these duties with my ever-firm intent, I was mindful that we might find a new parishioner among us. I was thwarted however, for though I cast an eye across the whole of my dwindling congregation, I could see no one that befitted the description of the new French doctor.

Indeed, I recognised every solitary sore-ridden face of my cursed flock, God save them. Each and every one a sinner, I am sure, but that is not for me to judge, but for Him.

And so, I blessed them all, and sent them scurrying back into the August sun with visions of Hell snapping at their behinds.

My labours for the Glory of God being at an end, I

decided that it was indeed something of a slight on the part of the doctor not to come to the Lord's house on a Sunday, and so I ventured to make a visit myself to the Hall, and introduce myself and the village to our newcomer.

As Rebecca comes to, she's dimly aware of a presence close by her, but when she opens her eyes, there's no one. At least, not at first.

She sits up and sees the girl there, standing by the cliff edge, looking down at the beach. The girl turns and smiles.

On second sight, she is still strange-looking; there's something elfin about her. Everything ends in points; her nose, her eyes, her chin, her lips, her fingers, the spikes of her long tresses of black hair.

'Are you okay?' she says.

Rebecca's still too muggy to think clearly.

'You were singing,' Ferelith remembers.

Rebecca gets to her feet gingerly.

'Careful. It was the shock. You don't want to get light-headed again.'

'Why are you standing so near the edge?' Rebecca asks.

'Same reason as you,' Ferelith says. 'It's irresistible, somehow, isn't it? To stand on the edge. Don't you think so?'

Rebecca listens to the curious way Ferelith speaks. Somehow old-fashioned and posh, but not posh-sounding.

'Who are you?'

'Ferelith. I told you that. But maybe you didn't hear because . . . You know, because.'

She gestures at the spot where Rebecca's sixteen years nearly ended.

Ferelith smiles. Rebecca notices more pointyness about her; her teeth, not quite a vampire's, but not far short. Already Rebecca feels there's something odd about this girl, though she wouldn't be able to put it into words. More than odd. Something darker than that, maybe.

'I saved your life!' Ferelith exclaims, dramatically, like a line from a bad film.

Rebecca doesn't smile.

'Why were you singing?'

'I'd better be going,' Rebecca says, not looking at Ferelith, more upset now by the embarrassment than the fact she could have been killed.

'Why? Where is there to go?'

Rebecca stops short. The girl has put her finger on something that she can't disagree with.

'That's a strange name,' she says.

'Ferelith? Why do you think so?'

'Well, not strange, then. But I haven't heard it before.'

26

Ferelith nods. 'Uncommon. That's what you meant to say. It means "stone bringer". It's Greek.'

Rebecca frowns.

'Your name means to tie or to bind. It's Hebrew.'

Rebecca frowns some more, and Ferelith moves away from the edge now.

'How do you know my name?' she asks.

Ferelith doesn't seem to feel the need to answer this.

'I like your crucifix,' she says instead. 'Who gave it to you?'

'How do you know anyone gave it to me?' Rebecca asks, but again Ferelith changes the subject.

'Why were you singing that? Dorothy?'

Rebecca shrugs.

'It popped into my head. That's all.'

'Do you know it almost got cut from the film? The most famous song in it, and they nearly left it out. Can you imagine that?'

Rebecca doesn't know what to say, finding the whole conversation too convoluted to understand.

'It's my favourite film. Is it yours? Or do you just like singing?'

'I played Dorothy at school,' Rebecca says before she knows what she's doing.

'You're the policeman's daughter, aren't you?'

Rebecca stiffens, wondering what the girl knows.

'You're his daughter, aren't you? I suppose you've just

come here for the summer. That's okay. Lots of people do that. Do you like it here? There's not much to do.'

'Not much? You can say that twice.'

Rebecca smiles.

'That wasn't so hard,' Ferelith says, and before Rebecca can ask what she means, adds, 'Yes. Very little to do. But I could show you some things, some places, if you like. We could be friends.'

She takes a couple of steps towards Rebecca, who stiffens again.

'No, I don't think so,' she says carefully. 'Thanks. Thanks for seeing I was okay.'

She turns, pushes through the bushes, and walks quickly back towards the village.

On the way back up The Street, she passes the pub. She looks at the sign, and where there was an angel, there is now a devil.

Another handsome figure, he's holding a black pitchfork, the tips of which are glowing red, the same colour as his skin. Though he's only visible from the waist up, the end of his forked tail curls behind him, and the fires of Hell rage all around. And unlike the angel Rebecca saw earlier, gazing up to the heavens, the devil is staring right at her, grinning.

Leering.

Now, Rebecca reads properly the name of the pub

painted on the front wall, large black ornate letters on the creamy white brick, and she understands. The sign has one picture on one side, and a different one on the other.

The Angel and The Devil.

1798, 8m, 23ð.

I am afraid.

O Lord! Look down on this, my Evening, and mend it, before Sunset comes forever.

I must record that I received a visitor this morning. As the sun shone fair on the Rectory gates, I spied a figure approaching, and at once knew it to be Dr Barrieux.

My hands trembled as I, finding Martha absent, opened the door to my home. He waited but briefly and yet would only stand two feet inside, and then invited me to dine at the Hall on the eve of the Lord's day, being the morrow.

1798, 8m, 25d.

God!

What I found there, at the Hall!

I cannot set it down tonight. I will take a bottle to my bed and that and God will aid my sleep, I pray.

God abandoned me in the short hours of the night, and I was sent a series of visions of Hell.

Who can measure this place?

It is infinite. The sky is brooding and red, the ground is hot, and sharp, and cuts the soles of the feet. The air is rent with the cries of the sinful as they receive their punishment, a flaming wind blows upon all sides causing madness, as of dogs.

What vast unnameable horrors are found!

I saw them all.

The sinners each tortured for all eternity according to their crime.

The lustful are cast upon spits and roasted on the fires of their former passions, and yea, are whipped by devils with the faces of dogs and the legs of the horse. They whip the lustful ones with leather thongs made of their own skin.

On another mountainside, are the gluttonous. Here they swim among the slurry from their own greed, forever drowning.

There lie the blasphemers, among piles of dry and dusty stones, each forced to eat the rock of truth they denied in life. They choke and gag as their teeth splinter and blood wells from their gums in never-ending streams.

I awoke from my torments in the dark morning, and slept no more.

Such are the visions of Hell.

But what then, is Heaven? How does the celestial realm appear? Why, Lord, is it so much harder to bring to sight than the other place?

Friday night and Rebecca considers her fate.

Should she re-read the stupid novel she finished this morning, or watch The Wizard of Oz, for some reason the only DVD in the house.

Her father's gone out. She doesn't know where. It seems he's out when she's in and she's out when he's in, a carefully orchestrated avoidance.

She's texted a few people back in Greenwich, but had no replies, which makes her feel like ancient history. She's texted Adam, as if everything is okay between them, telling him a little about Winterfold, a little about Ferelith, but he hasn't replied either. She's miles away from home, with all the freedom in the world, but nothing to do. Not even anyone else to do nothing with.

As she thinks that, the girl, Ferelith, pops into her head. She tries to pin down what she found so strange about her, but can't. It's more than the way she looks, though, she knows that. More than her thin pale skin and pixie eyes. It's something about what's inside, but Rebecca can't tell what that is yet.

Idly, she gets off the sofa and picks up the case for the

DVD, her face burning as she remembers being caught singing.

She wonders what the film is doing there. Her father won't have bought it, even he knows enough about her to know she's too old for that kind of stuff now. Maybe the people who own the house left it.

She wonders how long her dad will stay in this cottage, what will happen when they go back home, whether they'll have to run away again.

She stops herself, checking that she did actually think of it as running away. But what else would you call it?

The light in the cottage is failing as dusk falls, but rather than put a lamp on, she takes the DVD case to the window to read the label, and then promptly drops it as she sees a face outside pressed up against the glass.

Ferelith.

Her face disappears. A moment later there's a knock at the door.

Rebecca is halfway across the room when the door opens and Ferelith walks in.

'I came to see how you are,' she says brightly. 'After the other day. I didn't want you to think I didn't care.'

'You can't just come in here,' Rebecca says.

'Why not?' says Ferelith, but more like she's wondering aloud, than asking Rebecca. She makes an observation: 'Alone tonight.'

'Yes, so?' Rebecca snaps.

37

'Just wondering. No one likes being on their own, do they?'

'I'm fine,' Rebecca says, admitting to herself that she'd been looking forward to wallowing in her misery for a whole evening.

'Well, you say that, but . . .' Ferelith shrugs. 'Suit yourself.'

'I think you should go now,' Rebecca says, trying to sound calm. Ferelith sees the DVD on the floor and picks it up.

'Do you want to see a Munchkin commit suicide?'

'What?'

'I said, do you want to see a Munchkin hang himself? Really. It's a thing that happened on the set when they were filming. It's hidden away in the background but if you know where to look . . . There's stuff about it on the internet.'

Rebecca looks hard at Ferelith, trying to see into her and failing, though she senses that Ferelith can see straight through her.

'Are you trying to make fun of me?' is all she can think to say.

Ferelith smiles.

'No. The Munchkins were a bad lot, always drinking on set, and so on, and then on the other hand, they were really badly treated by the studio, and then one of them decided to protest against the shoot by pretending to

38

hang himself in the trees in the background. Only he messed it up and did it for real.'

'You're joking.'

'No. You can look on the net if you don't believe me. Better yet, I'll show you.'

She bends down to the DVD player, and grins up at Rebecca.

'Want to see?'

Rebecca suddenly laughs.

'Yeah. Why not? Show me a suicidal Munchkin.'

Ferelith fiddles with the remote.

'Of course, they didn't mean to leave it in. They had to re-shoot the scene and swear Judy and everyone else to secrecy. They say that's why she became an alcoholic, well, one reason anyway. But then when they edited the film someone put the wrong bit of film in and because it's so hard to see no one noticed for years. By then it was too late and the rest is history.'

Ferelith punches a few buttons and skips through the scenes.

'How do you know where it is?' Rebecca asks.

'My favourite film,' Ferelith says. 'Nearly there. Look, it's when they meet the Tin Man and then, there, as they go dancing down the yellow brick road. Look! Look there! Did you see it?'

Rebecca isn't sure what she's seen and says so.

39

'I'll play it again. Can you do repeat on this thing? Yes, there. Now look.'

It's hard to tell. There's definitely something swinging in the painted trees of the set, as Dorothy and the Tin Man and the Scarecrow skip away. The clip repeats time and time, a dark shape hovers on a branch and then appears to drop.

But an actor hanging himself?

Suddenly Rebecca bursts out laughing.

'What?' says Ferelith. 'He's killing himself and you're laughing!'

'I just thought what my friends would say if they knew I spent Friday night trying to see a Munchkin kill himself.'

40

I'm Not Dead

Supposing you wanted to prove something, something important. Supposing you wanted to prove, for argument's sake, that there is life after death.

Now you may say, I do not know of a single proven example of communication from beyond the grave. To the best of all human knowledge, it appears that we do not live on after death. And you might give me an example to make things simpler to understand. You might say that although you have not seen every crow in the whole world, every crow you have ever seen is black. Therefore the chances are very great that all crows are black. In fact, you have decided for a fact that all crows *are* black. Now of course, if someone could show you a white crow, everything would be overturned in a moment.

But all crows are black.

And in the same way, you conclude that no one lives after death. There is no 'other side'. There is no white crow.

But, supposing I said I had seen a white crow? Just one. A single white crow.

What then?

41

1798, 9m, 1d.

Today being the first of a new month brings with it thoughts of a new start, a new approach, and as sure as blood flows in my veins, I feel that this is a time of change, of the end of old things and the start of new ones. And yet Autumn is coming. I can smell it on the morning air, and Autumn signifies the approach of winter, of leaves on the ground, and bare branches in the air. It is death and decay.

It is a week now since I dined at the Hall, and I must finally acknowledge what I found, what we spoke of, and what manner of man is Dr Barrieux.

We ate in the large dining room, heavy drapes obscured the glass and made the place a gloomy pit.

We ate well, and drank, I am sore sick to confess, copiously, so that the meal became one long orgy of food, of drink, and of ideas.

And what ideas!

The doctor is a genius, I saw that at once, and I am immodest to suggest that I saw that he admired my skills with the soul as well.

It seems we have a great many thoughts in common, and as the food continued to be brought in, and as the wine continued to flow (God scourge me) like the rivers of the Holy Land, we approached each other; distant at first, but coming rapidly closer and closer.

I learned a little of the doctor's history, but there are things hidden from me that he would not speak of, and I was left to wonder at much. Of other members of family, I was not informed. He appears to be alone in the great rooms of Winterfold Hall, with only his serving staff on hand to minister to him.

At one moment or another he would refer tantalisingly to this name or that person, and some hints made me think that he was married. Or had been once.

What I did learn was that he was newly arrived from Paris, having served as a physician there for many years. I was to understand that he had survived the Reign of Terror, and the death of kings, despite working in a minor capacity in the court. He had then advised on the physical health of some of the revolutionaries themselves – Danton, Robespierre, Marat – again surviving where many of these did not.

And then, the trail of his tale grew vague, for all else I can recall of his ventures is his arrival in England, and his removal to Winterfold.

As we fell to talking of the great mysteries of life, we saw that we have a common purpose.

We will unite around that purpose, and our accomplishments will be great.

We will make a voyage to the unknown, and we will return with truth.

Over the weekend, Rebecca's father is preoccupied. At a late breakfast on Saturday the tension is unbearable, as they both torture each other with the clinks of cutlery on crockery. Rebecca tries to eat as fast as she can without making it look obvious, desperate to disappear back to her room.

She's standing up when her father speaks.

'Sorry,' he says. It's just enough to make her sit down again. She tells herself she doesn't hate him, what she hates is the situation he's got them in.

He doesn't continue, but gets up and fumbles in his briefcase, pulling out a newspaper article, torn from a larger sheet, folded and a bit faded.

She knows what it will be without needing to look, but she goes through the motions and unfolds it. She's right; it's one she's seen before, and she feels sick.

'Someone put it under the windscreen wiper. I guess I thought someone would find out.' He rubs his eyes with finger and thumb, and swears softly. 'I guess I thought someone would find out, just not so quickly.'

Rebecca gets to her feet and tries to put her arms

around him and hug him with the ease she had when she was little, but it doesn't come easily now.

He shakes his head.

'Plans for today?' he asks.

Rebecca shakes her head.

'Not sure.'

'Made any friends? You always had so many friends in London.'

'Not yet,' she says. 'No.'

She turns for the tiny staircase, heading for her room, when her father speaks again.

'We can get some more,' he says.

'More what?'

'More DVDs. If you're bored, we can get more, they only have a couple of old things at the shop, don't they?'

He sees the blank look on her face.

'The Wizard of Oz, I saw you bought it.'

A gentle tingle starts to inch up Rebecca's spine, heading for her neck.

'The DVD?' she says. 'It wasn't here when you rented the house?'

'No, nothing at all. I thought you bought it. Didn't you?'

'Oh, yes,' says Rebecca, 'No. That's right, I did.'

'You all right, Tiger?'

'Yes, more would be good,' says Rebecca, adding automatically, 'and don't call me Tiger.'

She vanishes upstairs, wondering exactly what it is she's feeling.

Fear? Fascination?

A little of both.

1798, 9m, 10ð.

The first day of the week brings a beginning to Winterfold Hall. After attending to some poor souls in the slum dwellings at the farm, and paying my regular courtesy to Widow Somers, I walked round by way of Long Lane, and through the wheat field, marvelling at a vast and raucous crowd of crows wheeling in the sky above me, to arrive at the Hall around the middle morning.

I am unsure as to what I expected to discover, but there seemed little to witness.

Having pulled on the bell cord and receiving no admittance, nor even reply, I retreated a few paces and, feeling the heat of the morning, sat on the lawn in front.

From time to time I fancied I heard subterranean rumblings, but dismissed these as the distant crashing of the waves on the beach, albeit some half-mile hence.

The morning wore on, and as I began to perceive an unheeded dampness from the grass through my cassock, I was about to leave, when the front door to the Hall swung open and a horde poured forth.

They looked as if they had come straight from Hell, a gang and gaggle of swarthy navvies, each stripped to the waist and sweating greatly, smeared with the detritus of the pit, wildly staggering for cleanliness of air, and daylight. They were a rum bunch, no doubt of that.

Behind them, somewhat more calmly, but not in his usual neat apparel, came the doctor.

He shouted to the workmen, bidding them to take breath, and water from the pump in the side yard.

Only then did Dr Barrieux apprehend my presence, and came to speak to me.

I enquired as to the state of progress.

– A fine start, Rector. Would you like to see?

I assured him I trusted his labours and his ministration, but he was like a boy excited by bees and would only insist that I see the developments with mine own eyes.

He spoke the truth.

– They arrived under darkness, he explained. So as not to arouse wonder in the town. They began early, and are you not impressed with their labours?

I was.

The doctor and I exchanged a few words, and then I returned to God's light, blinking, bidding the doctor farewell.

As I left I felt a great thirst, from the heat and the dirt, and though I would have had wine were it to hand, I turned my thoughts to the water pump the doctor had spoken of.

Unable to source its location, I turned to one of the navvies.

– My good fellow, I said, and bid him tell me where I could find water.

He stared at me as if he were stupid, or I, and did not answer me.

– Water? I said, pointing to my mouth.

He shook his head. I turned to another of the men, a hulking brute, and again he would not answer me, but this time pointed around to the far side of the hall.

Shaking my head, I made swift route to the pump, and saw two or three of the men gathered round it.

– Will you pump for me while I drink, man? I asked the nearest of them.

He bent to his task, but again said not a word.

I took a long drink, bathing my face in the cool liquid, and straightened.

The men stood watching me, and still none of them uttered a sound.

– What is wrong with you all? Do none of you have anything to say?

The nearest, who at least must have understood English, pointed to his mouth.

I shook my head in confusion, and so he opened his mouth, and showed me that he had no tongue, that at some point in his miserable life it had been cut out. He pointed to the man next to him, and the one next to him, and waved his hand at them, and they too opened their mouths to show that their organ of speech had also been forcibly removed.

Before I left, I went round every man in the gang, nine of them. Each and every one a mute.

Each and every one without the power of speech.

I wondered at Dr Barrieux, at what it was he intended; I wondered why he deemed a gang of mute labourers necessary to his work, and I marvelled at the power of the man to go to such lengths to ensure the success of his labours.

Four Sea Interludes – II

I spent a few days at home, but I didn't feel like talking to the others. I kept myself to myself. There were times when I needed them but since I turned sixteen I don't need them any more.

It had been fun with Rebecca, but I didn't want to push it. She seemed to me to be very shy, which is odd for someone so beautiful. And I . . . well, I'm me, so I thought I would leave her alone for a while.

But I began to grow itchy again, and so by Monday evening I decided to go out.

I walked down the lane from the house, hugging the shade by the high brick wall, because it had been a really hot afternoon, and the sun still shone fiercely, though it was gone six.

I walked along The Street, and as I passed The Mansion I slowed my pace, and risked glancing at the house from the corner of my eye. Maybe someone moved inside, maybe not, but I walked on, past the pub, and up into the woods by the snaking path, to the Lover's Seat. A walk I must have made a thousand times or more in my life, my life in Winterfold.

I waited.

It was even hotter at the Seat, if possible, for although the cool sea lay in front of me, there was not a breath of wind. The sea lay like a glassy pool, and even the waves breaking on the beach seemed without energy in the heat. It was what a sailor would have called a dead calm, and surrounded by the wall of trees and bushes, it was really, really hot.

I waited, but actually I didn't have long to wait.

I knew she was there behind me; I heard the rustle in the bushes, too big for a walker's dog, and I heard the rustle stop suddenly as she must have seen I was there.

I waited, and when she came like a timid deer into the Lover's Seat, I turned, pretending to be surprised.

'Oh,' she said, 'Sorry. I didn't know . . .'

She paused, expecting me to say something, looking for an excuse to back out again. I wasn't going to give her one.

'That's okay,' I said. 'It's a free country. I'm not doing anything anyway. Sit down.'

I patted the grass beside me and she came over.

She sat further away than necessary, as if she was scared of me, so I tried to make her feel better.

'How are you finding Winterfold, then?'

She shrugged. It was just one of many little gestures she had that somehow made her even more beautiful.

'Quiet. It's really quiet here,' she said, and laughed, quickly and briefly.

I smiled.

'That's about it.'

I looked out to sea.

'But you know, once upon a time…'

'Are you going to tell me a story?' she said, seriously.

'Yes, I guess I am,' I said. I started again. 'Once upon a time, this was the biggest town for a hundred miles around.'

'That's not possible.'

'It's true. You can read all about it in the museum if you like. Of course, it was quite a long time ago.'

'How long?' Rebecca asked, tilting her head on one side, so her hair hung across one eye. Another one of those mannerisms.

'About eight hundred years, give or take. It was a big town, with thousands of people, dozens of streets, hundreds of houses, about ten churches.'

'So what happened to it?'

'The sea's been eating away at the coast here for centuries. It started with a big storm in 1218; the harbour flooded over into the town and by the next day half the town had gone. It's been much slower since then, but still it goes on, bit by bit. Even in my lifetime. I've seen three houses lost, abandoned to the sea, and then fall over the cliff bit by bit.'

'That's incredible.'

'It's great,' I said. 'I love it. The current rate of collapse is two metres a year, on average. Sometimes more, sometimes less.'

'How do you know all this stuff?' Rebecca asked.

It wasn't really worth answering that; I find it boring to explain, so I gave her an answer that suited me.

'I just remember stuff easily.'

That was the best way of putting it. Before she could speak again, I had an idea.

'Listen, it will be dusk soon, but there's still time. I could take you to the church. Then you'll really get an idea of what's happening in Winterfold.'

She hesitated for a moment, but only a moment. I wondered what was happening in her head. What she was thinking, what she was thinking about me.

'Okay,' she said. 'That would be good.'

'Excellent,' I said. 'Actually, evening's the best time to visit the church.'

'Why's that?'

'You'll see.'

'I didn't even know there was a church here.'

'Like I said, there were lots. There's only one left now, and it's on the other side of these woods, further along the cliff. You'll love it.'

I stood up and put my hands out to pull Rebecca up from where she sat.

She saw me holding out my hands. She stood up by herself, but she smiled.

She was happy enough.

'Come on then. Show me the church.'

So we went, by the snaking path through the woods that clung to the edge of the cliff, through the trees, each tree waiting for its time to come, the time when it would meet the advancing sea, and fall into the water with a tumble of root and branch.

The two girls make their way through the thickets of this scrubby wood – a twenty-minute walk, but only fifty strides wide, with farmland to the right and the cliff to the left, as they head south along the coast.

More than once, Ferelith stops and points.

'Look! See that way, there. That path used to go somewhere, and now it just falls off the edge. Into the sea. Splosh!'

Ferelith chats about this and that, explaining the history of the village, like a textbook, Rebecca thinks. Ferelith is certainly unusual, and intelligent. Maybe very intelligent. Rebecca wonders about the DVD, and whether she should ask straight out if Ferelith put it in their house. She decides not to.

Again Ferelith stops.

'I want to show you something,' she says, pushing off the path and into the undergrowth once more. 'Come on!'

Rebecca watches her go, and then pushes in after her. The branches snap back, whipping her cheeks.

'Ow!' she cries, but Ferelith doesn't stop, head down, fighting a couple of brambles that have hooked her.

She drops onto her hands and knees and Rebecca drops beside her.

'Ow!' she says again.

'Yes,' says Ferelith, 'but look.'

In front of them is a gravestone. Just one, overgrown by weeds, covered in moss. Behind it through the trees lurks the bright and sunny cliff edge, maybe three metres away.

'This is the luckiest man in Winterfold. Well, in this churchyard anyway.'

'What churchyard?' Rebecca asks, feeling slow. 'It's just weeds and bushes.'

'It is now, but this was the churchyard of St James's. It's not the one we're going to look at. That one's still standing. All that's left of St James's is this one gravestone. All the rest have fallen into the sea. So this is the luckiest man in the churchyard. Look, you can just see his name.'

Ferelith traces her pointed fingertip across the letters, hard to read through the lichen, but still legible.

'Robert Eyatt, Departed this earth, July 30th 1752.'

'That's in four days' time,' Rebecca says.

Ferelith nods.

'This year, maybe next. No more than three, and he'll be in the sea too.'

'That's creepy,' Rebecca says, but even as she says it, she finds it fascinating too.

'I think it's fun,' Ferelith says, sensing Rebecca's interest. 'After a big storm, I run along the beach in the morning and see what I can find.'

'Find?'

'From the graves. I've found some amazing things over the years. I can show you sometime, if you like.'

'Thanks,' says Rebecca, but her voice is empty. Is this what she finds unsettling about Ferelith? Some foreshadowing in her, some foreshadowing of death?

'Come on,' Ferelith says, getting back to her feet. 'This is the only grave of St James's left, but there are still loads at St Mary's. It's getting dark, we should hurry.'

They retrace their haphazard route through the undergrowth to the relative ease of the path. In another few minutes they come to the end of the wood. The path turns inland and joins the main footpath that the dog walkers use, and runs parallel to the cliff for a short while. Then it stops, and turns up a slight rise.

Here, Ferelith ducks underneath some yellow tape strung across the path, preventing access to the churchyard. It's the sort of tape police put around a crime scene; she's seen her father with it, but this is not a crime scene. The tape has some writing on it, but in the dark she can't make it out.

Dusk has fallen, and the sun is out of sight beneath the horizon now. Still, there's enough light for Rebecca to see the shape of a large church rearing from the ground.

'This is St Mary's,' Ferelith says, 'and it's the best church in the world.'

Rebecca doubts that. When she was little her parents took her to lots of places: Moscow, Venice, Chartres. So she's seen some amazing churches and cathedrals and been equally amazed and bored by them all.

'Really?' she says, not that interested. They're standing in the churchyard, and there are indeed plenty more graves around them. Ferelith glides away in the gathering darkness towards the front west door of the church.

'Oh, you wait!' she cries, and as Rebecca follows, Ferelith grabs the huge iron handle, and wrestles with it.

'It'll be locked,' Rebecca calls.

'No point,' Ferelith says.

'Why not?'

Ferelith has the door moving now, and puts her insubstantial weight behind it, leaning with her shoulder to get it open. The door swings wide as Rebecca catches up with her.

'That's why,' says Ferelith.

'Oh,' says Rebecca, unable to find anything smarter to say.

She's looking through the door, but she's not looking into the church, instead, she's looking through it.

She's looking through it, because the church has no

back. She can see the nave, the aisles, there are even pews between the columns, and there's a roof to the columns, but the whole eastern end of the church is missing.

What she's looking at is the last glow of light from the sunset, the dusky sky, some wisps of cloud, and an evening star.

Where the pulpit should be, the moon hangs low in the sky, as if rising out of the sea like a bathing goddess.

'Oh,' Rebecca says again.

'I told you,' Ferelith says, and laughs. 'The end fell away about five years ago. It's been pretty stable since then, but they've stopped having services in here. Which I think is a shame. Because . . .'

She runs down the aisle, dancing like a ballerina, and before Rebecca can guess what she's going to do, leaps onto the altar.

'Because I think it's better now!' she cries.

'You shouldn't do that!' Rebecca calls, running to stand by the altar on which Ferelith is now dancing to some unheard tune.

'Why not?' she calls.

'Because it's . . . wrong,' Rebecca says, aware of how pointless that sounds.

Ferelith stops dancing. She puts her hands on her hips and looks down at Rebecca.

'Before this church closed for business, four old

ladies and a dog made up the whole congregation. I really don't think it's much missed. The eastern end of the church is the sacred end, the end that looks towards the Holy Land. But the eastern end is gone, and now it looks towards something truly magnificent! The sea! This church is a temple to the sea!'

Rebecca shakes her head.

'You're crazy,' she says, but Ferelith's mood is too infectious.

'Look!' Ferelith says. 'Isn't it amazing? You look that way and the stained glass is still there. You look that way, and it's just sky and sea.'

Rebecca looks at the windows, and in the dusk she makes out a scene from the Easter story. Ferelith notices.

'It's horrible, isn't it?'

She sounds subdued all of a sudden. Her smile has gone.

'What?' Rebecca asks.

'That story. How they crucify him. It's gruesome. Don't you think?'

'I suppose so. I've never looked at it like that. When I think of Easter I think of eggs and bunnies and chocolate and . . .'

'Yes, but what's Easter all about? A dead guy on a cross.'

'Maybe.'

'You know what the really sad thing is?' Ferelith asks.

She stands on the altar as if she's preaching.

'What?'

'Well,' she says. 'He died on the Friday, and rose from the dead on the Sunday, right?'

'So? What's so sad about that?'

'Well,' says Ferelith. 'He missed nearly all the bank holiday weekend.'

She starts giggling again, and tilts her head to the night sky.

'Come on, come up and join me,' she says, and Rebecca can't resist any more.

Rebecca reaches out and Ferelith pulls her onto the ancient stone table, and they both begin to dance.

'What are you dancing to?' Rebecca asks.

'None of your business!' Ferelith says with mock outrage. 'What about you?'

'I'm not sure,' Rebecca says, 'but you know, this is totally wrong. It might not even be safe.'

'Do you care?' Ferelith asks, not breaking step.

Rebecca can't even see the edge of the cliff now. There's a gaping hole where the sanctuary should be, and very, very near, she can hear the sound of the waves breaking at the foot of the cliffs.

Suddenly Ferelith grabs Rebecca round the waist, a hand on each hip, and keeps dancing. Rebecca doesn't stop her, and lets her touch her, though she doesn't touch back. Not yet. Ferelith holds her gaze for a long time, before asking her question again.

'Well,' she says. 'Do you care?'

Rebecca thinks. She's dancing in the dusk on the altar of a dead church that now only worships the sea, and suddenly she realises it's not the sort of thing she will do every day of her life.

She tosses her hair, smiling, and throws her hands in the air. She leans back and Ferelith has to take all her weight to stop her from tumbling off the stone table.

'No!' Rebecca shouts. 'I guess not. I don't care!'

Suddenly there's a flicker of light at the door, a torch beam arrows across the pews, and a voice is shouting.

'Who's that? Who's there? Hey!'

'Run!' shouts Ferelith, and they jump from the altar, and duck around the open end of the church, closer still to a near vertical cliff edge that could slip away at any moment.

They don't stop running till they're back in Winterfold. Safe.

66

1798, 9m, 15d.

I was born among a set of foul heathen thinkers, and in that sect I was without God and knew not of God until my eleventh year on the earth, when a plague of vicious ills was enough to wipe the heathens away, leaving me alone. It was a miracle. I came to see it that way, in time.

Unknowing of my true place in the world, and destitute, I came upon a house of God, and they, seeing my plight, taught me the truth of the world, and of God's love, and of his terrible wrath.

And thus, though I came late to the Truth, did I come upon it fervently, and do now, I believe, hold the Truth more strong than any other man.

1798, 9m, 16ð.

Today is the Lord's day, and after I had undertaken my duties of worship, I ended the day in solemn contemplation of my lot.

As I now approach the far end of my life, certain thoughts raise themselves above others.

More and more, my dreams are haunted by visions of a dire and dreadful nature.

My preaching today, as often these days, hounded the sinful and the wicked. Even as I stood in the pulpit, I scourged the wrong-doers below me with a thousand lashes of my tongue.

And yet, O God, am I any better than any of the wicked of my congregation? And when my time comes, what will be my judgement?

Where will I spend eternity?

Catholic Day

We all make choices, thousands of them, each and every day. Many are so small that we're barely aware of making them: which knickers shall I wear today? What shall I have for lunch? Shall I leave that light on, or not? Which foot shall I put first on the threshold?

But some of our choices are bigger, not massive, but bigger, and they have an impact on the people around us: shall I help that old lady with her shopping, or not? Shall I say something kind to you when I meet you? Shall I laugh at your ideas, shall I walk through the world gently, or shall I push everyone aside?

And then there are the biggest choices, ones which don't come along every day, but once in a while, and which are the stuff of fears and worries and of major turns in the road; these are the choices we make for good, or ill, and they determine our future, and the future of those around us.

It's these choices that interest me the most.

Ferelith knocks on Rebecca's door at two o'clock next day, as they've arranged.

Rebecca's father opens the door, and raises an eyebrow at the girl standing there. He's still finding it hard getting used to living in the country, and last night, walking late in Hall Lane he heard someone mucking about in the ruined church. Probably just kids getting kicks, but he resented having to be a policeman when he no longer is. He'd mentioned it to Rebecca, but she'd just given him a look and turned away.

The girl at the door is odd. She's a bit overdressed given the continual heat the summer is throwing at everyone, but there's something more than that he can't place, not just that she's dressed entirely in black, which looks strange in the height of summer.

'Are you Rebecca's friend?' he asks.

'Ferelith, yes,' she says, and holds out a hand.

'John Case,' Rebecca's father says, thrown slightly that there is still a teenage girl in the world who knows how to introduce herself properly.

He shakes her hand, and stands aside, grabbing his bag

from the small table by the door.

'I'm just off,' he says, 'but Rebecca's upstairs. You can go and find her.'

'What do you do, Mr Case?' asks Ferelith as she steps into the house.

'I'm a Detective Insp—' he stops himself, rewinds slightly. 'I'm . . . doing a spot of gardening. Here and there. I'm just here for the peace and quiet.' He stops, wondering why he's bothering to tell her this.

'Absolutely,' says the girl, and wanders into his house, leaving him to close the door and head over to his car, trying to work out why he feels he's just been defeated in some way.

They chat as they stroll down to the beach, towels over their shoulders.

Rebecca carries a plastic bag with some bottles of water and a couple of apples, Ferelith has a CD player, old and battered but loud-looking.

They crunch their way onto the shingle and Ferelith groans.

'Let's get away from the tourists a bit, yes?' she says, and without waiting for a reply, heads to the left and away from the families, couples and gangs of teenagers clogging up the nearest stretch of beach.

The sun burns, and Rebecca pulls her floppy straw sunhat down across her face.

'Did you bring sun cream?' she asks.

'Put it on at home,' says Ferelith. 'Factor One Thousand to keep my coffin-like complexion. Didn't you?'

'No,' says Rebecca, unable to inspect Ferelith's pale white skin. 'I'll go back and get some.'

She hurries home and by the time she gets back to where they were, she can't see Ferelith. Then she spots a speck of black a long way off down the beach. She heads in that direction, but as she gets close, and finds the towel and the stereo, she can't see Ferelith. She catches sight of someone bobbing around in the water. The figure raises an arm and waves, then dives and starts swimming steadily back to shore.

Rebecca watches her approach, smearing sun cream on herself as she does so, and then as Ferelith gets to the shallows and stands up, Rebecca realises that she's naked.

As soon as she's out of the water, she starts to run up the beach. Rebecca looks around frantically. There are people in plain sight, but maybe they're all too far way to see or care.

Ferelith arrives, swearing comically with each painful footstep on the shingle, and grabs her towel, pulling it round her.

'Coming in?' she says, panting, shaking her wet hair out.

'You haven't got anything on,' Rebecca says.

Ferelith raises an eyebrow, maybe about to say something sarcastic, but all she says is, 'Nicer that way. So? Coming?'

'Yes, but I'm keeping this on,' Rebecca says, pinging the strap of her swimming costume.

'Suit yourself,' Ferelith says. 'Are you shy?'

'Something like that. I just don't take my clothes off

in full view of half the world.'

Ferelith cocks her head on one side.

'Supposing I dared you to?'

Rebecca actually laughs at that.

'What do you mean?'

'If I dared you to do it, would you do it then?'

'No. I wouldn't. What difference does that make?'

Ferelith drops her towel, and runs back to the water.

'Maybe a lot,' she calls as she goes.

'Wait,' says Rebecca, but Ferelith is gone.

Rebecca pulls off her shorts and T-shirt, but keeping her swimming costume firmly on, she tiptoes down to the water, feeling faintly disappointed, though like her father, she can't work out exactly why.

Heaven is a field of summer-ripened wheat, upon which the sun always shines, but there is a cool brook nearby to quench your thirst.

No.

Heaven is a pasture of green, with apple trees, and young lambs nibbling the grass beneath them.

No.

Heaven is a vast white cloud where the angels sit, playing gentle and sweet music, reciting tragic poetry to each other.

No.

Heaven is a forest glade in which a thousand pretty girls lie in wait, each one sitting on a freshly opened barrel of wine.

NO!

Why is it so hard to envisage a blissful afterlife? Why is it so hard? Try as I might, I do not feel that anything I can think of even begins to approach the true nature of God's celestial realms. Why is this? Do I find it easier to conjure the other place to mind because that is where I am heading?

O Lord, let me mend my ways while I still can, and

while I still have time, let me see the truth of what lies on the other side of the veil!

But, Lord, I swear upon your son's name, that if you will not show me, then Dr Barrieux and I shall find out for ourselves.

Today I was at the Hall, and the doctor and I spoke long and hard upon our quest. I have recorded before that our quest is to be a voyage into the unknown, but only today did this miraculous Frenchman reveal his full methods to me. We talked, nay, argued for an hour and more and then with a curse, he threw his hands in the air, would speak no more, and took me by the hand.

Holy God!

What I saw!

For when our speaking came to a close, Dr Barrieux led me into the darkest bowels of Winterfold Hall, and there I beheld the dreadful apparatus with which our voyage will be made.

1798, 9m, 19d.

Last night I was plagued by night terrors. I scarce ever saw myself so weak and bereft as this night, and I could find no rest.

I rose at four in the morning, abandoning the torture of my bed, and stumbled into the night, and the fresh air revived my senses.

Deciding me to take a walk, I wandered the streets of Winterfold, and before I knew it, my feet were leading me to the Hall.

As I approached, I saw why they had led me there.

Despite the hour, a candle burned in a room on the ground floor, at the side of the house. I know this room to be the doctor's study, and I made my way to the window and peered in.

There sat the doctor, poring over some accounts I fancied. I tapped on the window and far from seeming surprised, the doctor turned his head, squinted, then lifted a hand and beckoned me in.

I met him at the kitchen door and he led me into the drawing room, where the remains of a fire glowed in the grate.

I beheld the doctor. A man of forty or fifty years on the earth, I could not tell which. His wig sat on the desk before him, and now I saw that he still owned a fine head of black hair, but peppered through with grey, as of one who has seen the troubles of the world. His skin is pallid, yet smooth, and I suppose he has kept indoors for most of his time. He has a fine nose, and strong eyebrows, and his stare is most fixed.

He poured me a glass of port, and another of the same for himself, and bid me sit at the fireside.

I did as I was invited, and suddenly, with one sip of the drink at this early hour, began to feel the weariness within me. But the doctor was speaking, speaking of matters both great and small. He spoke of his life, and I tried to heed him, but it became hard to distinguish wakefulness from sleep, and I drifted in and out of the room, my mind like a phantom in the dark.

He spoke of his time in Paris. He had not been born there, but in some place to the south, a place of sunflower fields and walnut trees, he said, but I do not remember if he gave it a name. As a young man he studied natural philosophy, and his studies brought him inevitably to the great city of Paris, with all its philosophers, thinkers, poets, painters, musicians and lovers.

He sampled some of each.

I had grown extreme drowsy, but I know he was speaking of things close to him. All I can recall, is this. He got up from his chair, and went to a table in the corner of the room, returning with a small pair of portraits, two ovals in one frame. Though my ears seemed to have closed down, my eyes beheld a young woman, and a little girl. The woman was beautiful, with curling tumbling black hair, and the complexion of milk. She gazed from her portrait as if amused by something.

In the other half of the frame sat the young girl. She is perhaps eight, a frail and weak-looking thing.

They are mother and daughter, it is clear, and I did not perceive what the doctor was telling me, but he leaned over the chair in which I sat, holding out the portraits, urging me to look.

Then I saw that tears were freely running down his face.

One fell from the doctor's cheek to mine, and I wiped it away.

He said one word, of French, and it is a word that even I know.

– Mort!

— *Tuesday 27th July* —

Rebecca and Ferelith swim and sunbathe, sunbathe and swim all afternoon. The sun is unrelenting, the sky is blue from one horizon to the other, the waves shush on the shingle, the tide slowly, slowly edges in, then by mid afternoon halts and starts its retreat.

A group of three boys loiter nearby. They're a little older than the girls, and Rebecca is relieved that Ferelith covers herself up a bit more as they come by. They make a few blunt remarks about the girls, and what they'd like to do with them, but soon get bored when neither shows any sign of reacting.

'Idiots,' mutters Ferelith from under her hat. 'Is there any more water?'

'All gone,' Rebecca mutters dreamily. She's been thinking about her life in London, feeling sorry for herself, enjoying feeling sorry for herself, and marvelling at how different things feel in Winterfold. Until Ferelith spoke she'd been imagining that it was Adam lying next to her on the beach, talking to her about music as he often did, tracing the line of her eyebrows with a fingertip, and the line of her lips.

The spell is broken.

She sits up and gazes out to sea. It shimmers in the heat haze, and she can taste that her lips are salty from the sea water.

'We could go to that café,' she nods her head back to the beach car park.

'No way,' says Ferelith. 'It stinks in there. Let's go to the pub and have some chips.'

'The pub?'

'Yeah, the pub. Haven't you been there yet? It smells too, but in a better way.'

'You're really selling it,' Rebecca says.

They pull their clothes back on lazily, and saunter back into the village and into The Angel and The Devil. Ferelith chooses a quiet corner away from the bar, and a dumpy girl comes over, notepad in hand.

She clearly knows Ferelith, but also clearly has no intention of saying any more than is necessary to her.

'Two Cokes and a bowl of chips,' Ferelith says, and the girl scribbles on her pad, not troubling to hide her scorn. She stomps off and Ferelith adds, 'Think you can remember that?'

'Shhh!' hisses Rebecca. 'She'll spit in your Coke or something.'

'She wouldn't have the brains to even think of that.'

'Doesn't she like you?'

'She was in my year at school.'

'Was? Did she get excluded for being too grumpy?'

'No, she didn't leave. She doesn't like me because she's still there and I'm not.'

'What do you mean? Did you get excluded?'

'No, I left.'

The dumpy girl returns with the Cokes and pretty much slams them onto the table top, spilling some.

'Thanks, Melanie,' Ferelith says, insincerely.

Melanie has already plodded away and is trying to flirt with some boys at the bar, maybe even the ones who'd passed them on the beach earlier. They look over from time to time, one of them catches Rebecca's eye.

'What do you mean, you left?' she asks, looking away.

'Just that. Two years ago.'

'You left school when you were fourteen?'

This raises so many questions in Rebecca's head that she doesn't know which one to ask first.

'I'd had enough of school. I did my A-levels, I couldn't go to university, I came home, my mum went mad, Dad left. That's all there is to know.'

'Wait, wait, you did your A-levels when you were fourteen?'

'Yes. After that I couldn't be bothered any more.'

'And you said, your mum . . .'

'My mum went mad. Listen, I don't want to talk about it, okay.'

She sips her Coke and looks out of the window.

'Then maybe you shouldn't have mentioned it in the

first place,' Rebecca says quietly, wondering why she feels the need to be tetchy. Maybe it's just the heat that's got to her.

Melanie brings the bowl of chips over, and slopes off again. They're undercooked and soggy and Ferelith fetches lots of ketchup and vinegar.

'The Angel's finest fare,' she says, drowning the chips. 'Enjoy.'

They start eating slowly, thoughtfully.

'I'm sorry,' Rebecca says. Then, 'But where do you live? Who do you live with if you don't have any parents?'

Ferelith shrugs.

'I live with this bunch of losers. It's sort of a commune type thing. Big house at the end of the village, in Long Lane. They're all drop-outs of one kind or another. Nobody has any money, everyone gets by somehow.'

'Sounds great, really…what's the word?'

'The word you're thinking of is bohemian.'

'Yes, that's it.'

'But it isn't. It's a hole.'

Ferelith falls silent again, and Rebecca hunts for something to say.

Almost accidentally, she hits the right thing.

'This place is nice,' she says, meaning the pub. And it is, it's old world Englishness, the real thing, not reconstructed to look like it by some marketing men. 'But the name is so weird.'

Ferelith lights up.

'It's brilliant, isn't it?'

'I've heard of pubs called the The Angel, but The Devil, too? That's odd.'

'It's . . . uncommon,' she says, and grins. Then she leans in close to Rebecca and utters in a mock stage whisper, 'But do you want to know the truth behind the name? Yes? Do you dare hear the truth?'

'Ooh, Stop it, you're scaring me,' says Rebecca, playing along. Then she forces herself to look serious. 'Very well. Do your worst! Tell me the awful and horrible truth behind it all!'

Ferelith nods.

Rebecca sees something flicker in her friend's dark eyes, but she cannot tell what it is. Ferelith puts her hand on Rebecca's, and their eyes meet.

'Okay,' she says, glancing at the others by the bar. 'But not here. There's somewhere better we can go.'

The Warning

I was glad to get out of the pub, anyway.

I could see Melanie was up for making trouble, and on another day I might have enjoyed it, but I was thinking about Rebecca. I could see Tom Halter and his mates looking at her too often, as well.

It was still hot, so we took the dog track beside the woods, past St Mary's again.

'You're right,' Rebecca said, pausing at the churchyard gate.

I said, 'I usually am,' or some similarly lame thing. 'But what about, this time?'

'The church is better at night.'

I nodded. She was reading the words on the tape across the path. She tutted.

'You probably don't want to look at that either, then,' I said, pointing at the 'Danger: Keep Out' sign just inside the gate.

She read it.

'Yes, well, "entering the site" very probably is "liable to lead to injury and the danger of death." You know, I seem to remember we danced on the altar. Isn't that . . . what's the word?'

'Blasphemous?'

'Yes. Isn't that blasphemous?'

'Well, I don't know the exact rules, but I would think they probably include dancing on altars in the list of bad things. But then, I think it really depends on whether you believe in God. Don't you?'

Rebecca didn't say anything. She seemed thoughtful, and I let her have her thoughts. For a while at least.

I went on along the path round the far end of the churchyard, and she followed.

She asked me if I believed in God.

'I asked first,' I said.

'No, you didn't,' she said, and we argued, until she gave in.

'I'm not sure,' she said eventually. 'I've never really thought about it.'

'That's it?' I asked. 'All that fuss for "I've never really thought about it?"'

She said she was just being honest, then she asked me again if I believed in God. I looked at the crucifix around her neck before answering, trying to think how to reply.

'What do you think?' I said eventually, and walked off.

'That's not fair,' she said. 'That's not a proper answer.'

Then we argued about that for a bit until I think she forgot that she hadn't had an answer at all.

I asked her if she had a boyfriend back in London.

What she said was funny.

No, what she *did* was funny.

'Yes,' she said, but she took forever to say it. Then there

was another pause and I think she expected me to say something. I didn't, I just waited for her to talk again.

'He's called Adam.'

I thought about Adam. I had a picture of him in my head straight away, though I knew nothing about him. But I could see him. I knew the type, just a stupid dull boy, like Tom and his mates in the pub. She didn't need him. I mean Rebecca didn't need an idiot like that, she needed someone better.

'So what's the problem?'

'Pardon?' Rebecca said.

'So what's the problem?' I repeated. 'I can tell there's a problem.'

'The problem is I'm stuck here.'

She looked really angry.

I thought she was going to be sick, or yell at me, but all she did was stop walking for a second, laugh once, and then start walking again.

I took that to be the end of the conversation.

We came to the turning where the path runs back inland to find the main road again, and Rebecca was heading in that direction when I called her back.

'No, this way,' I said pointing over the wall into the grounds of the Hall. I was trying not to think about Adam.

I saw that look in her eye again.

'Isn't that trespassing?'

'Not really,' I said. 'Someone would have to live there for it to be trespassing, wouldn't they?'

'Maybe,' she said. 'Where are we, anyway?'

We were at Winterfold Hall.

There's a bit of wall that's half collapsed and it's easy to climb over. I hopped over, and waited for her to follow, and when she did, we walked through the grounds of the Hall to my favourite place. The grounds are really wild and it's a great place to walk. You can see the remains of the old paths that lead through the trees, but they're all overgrown and the surface has decayed and crumbled over the years.

Weeds and vines cling to everything, ivy drips from every branch, and it's always deathly quiet in there, it's even hard to hear the sea, though it's not far away. Closer to the house itself, the jungle gives out and it's just tall grass and weeds up to the front door, but that wasn't where I was headed.

One of the paths leads through the trees to a funny little footbridge, which crosses a sunken path that runs straight from the Hall to the sea. I wonder where it used to lead, because now it just drops off into the sea not long after it goes under the bridge, which is beautiful and old. It's a honey colour when it's dry, but when it rains it goes dark grey, and the moss and lichen make it slippery. Then you have to be careful.

I often come and sit on the bridge; in fact, as I told Rebecca, I come and sit here almost every evening in the hot weather. And if it's raining, I still come and sit, but underneath.

And though there'd been no sign of rain for weeks, and none in sight, I felt it more appropriate to sit underneath to tell Rebecca my story.

'This is cute,' she said, and made a big fuss about finding something dry to sit on. I threw my towel on the ground.

'That's bone dry now,' I said. 'So be a good girl and listen to my story.'

She smiled, but not with her eyes as usual, because she was wondering if I was kidding or not, which was interesting in itself, because I wasn't sure either. I allowed myself a moment to stare at her face; those freckles that made her lightly tanned skin seem even more perfect. Her hair held up at the back of her neck, strands tumbling onto her shoulders.

Then I told her the legend of Winterfold Hall.

Most people in Winterfold can tell it, but they'll do it really badly, or forget bits, and even if they get it all right, they tell it as though it's just a silly story.

But I think it's a great story. It goes back a few hundred years, I'm not sure exactly, because some say it's only two hundred, whereas others say four or even five. Whatever, everyone agrees that Winterfold Hall has always been a strange place, and that strange things have always happened there. In the museum, you can read about it. It says that the original medieval Manor House was built on the site of worship of some pagan cult or other, but I don't know how they know that. They say the first Lords of the Manor built a house and a chapel on the site to try and stamp out the last vestiges of superstition. That's what it says in the museum, 'Last vestiges of superstition'. By building a church.

Anyway, that first house and chapel are long gone, and the one that's there now has some medieval bits, and some later bits, Georgian and Victorian.

So, whenever it was, a few hundred years back, the house was bought by a strange man, a magician, some say, or others, a wizard. Like there's a difference.

Even then the house had been empty for years, but this new owner soon had lights burning in the windows, at all times of day and night.

The magician's name was Barrow, and even though Barrow was all alone, just him with no family or anything, he had many visitors, at ungodly hours.

Rumours started spreading as to what was going on in the house, and still the visitors came.

And rumours started going around that the people who went in never came out at all.

So one day, a small boy from the village (why is it always a small boy in these kinds of stories?) decided to try and find out what was happening, and one evening, he sneaked into the Hall through the kitchens, and hid behind a curtain in the entrance hall.

Eventually, he fell asleep, and when he woke up it was

very far into the night, and dark. He listened from behind his curtain, because right at that moment, Barrow the wizard was welcoming a new guest to the Hall.

'Are you sure?' Barrow asked the guest, and the guest, from the sound of his voice, an old man, announced that he was.

But Barrow was not satisfied, and repeated his question, not once, but twice more.

'Are you sure? Are you sure?'

And each time the old man said he was.

'Very well,' said Barrow, 'I have asked you three times,' and he led the way into the depths of the house. The small boy followed unseen, and was in time to glimpse Barrow and the old man enter a small room in the very centre of the house. Barrow carried a candelabra, with five lighted candles on it. All the boy could see as the pair entered was a large chair standing in the middle of an otherwise apparently empty room, but a few minutes later Barrow left the room, without the candelabra.

He turned and locked the door, and then disappeared along a passageway. The boy didn't see him again that night. But it took him a long time to get up the courage to go and spy through the keyhole.

When he did, his eyes must have opened as wide as saucers, for this is what he saw. The old man was tied to a chair by thick and strong ropes, and by the light from the candles, the boy could see that the chair was some rather

91

strange apparatus, bolted to the floor. The candelabra stood on the floor a few feet in front of the man, otherwise, the room was empty.

The boy waited. And waited, and waited some more, and nothing happened.

He went back to his hiding place, and must have dozed, because he woke suddenly and rushed back to the keyhole. The man still sat there.

Two of the candles had gone out, and the third was guttering, almost gone too.

And the man was whispering. Whispering something over and over again, the same five words, but so quietly and quickly that the boy could not hear what he said.

Then the third candle went out, and just a few minutes later, the fourth. The old man kept repeating the same five words, again and again and again, like an incantation of his own. And now the whispering grew louder, and the boy heard what he was saying:

"The angel or the devil, the angel or the devil, the angel or the devil . . ."

Then there was a long wait, a terrible, long, long wait, while the fifth candle flickered and spluttered, nearly died and came back to life, and without warning went out. The room was plunged into darkness.

Then came a different voice.

'Are you a God-fearing man?'

That was all, and a few seconds later, there came a

terrible scream, which sent the boy running from the Hall.

Barrow had discovered the power to summon spirits, right there, in Winterfold Hall, but whether the spirit was good, an angel, or bad, a devil, depended on the person.

If the person had led a good life, and was going to Heaven, they'd be sent an angel, to calm them and soothe them and tell them Heaven was waiting.

But if they had sinned, then a devil would come and warn them to repent while they still could, filling their minds with the horrors of Hell.

And if they had sinned so badly, that there was nothing they could do to redeem themselves, then the Devil would take them there and then, and drag them off, screaming all the way to Hell.

It's quite a horrible story.

I love it.

1798, 9m, 22d.

O my folly!

For even the greatest part of my life has been spent in the care and consideration of the bodies of other men, to the exclusion of care for mine own, and in so doing I have exacerbated the neglect of my soul.

Lord, mend me!

Save me!

Before it is too late.

1798, 9m, 23d.

Hell is an infinite plane, for the sinners of the world are without measure. I know its roads and its byways, and they are all horror.

Come walk with me for a time (I will give you wooden shoes to prevent the ground from burning you) and we may spend a spell with the Devil and his uncountable wicked apprentices, each one assigned to torture one damned soul for all eternity.

With each arrival in Hell, in a crashing ball of flame that thunders to the ground like a plunging cannonball, the Lord of Darkness spawns a new demon from a vast slunky pond of evil. The thing crawls out like a babe from a blanket, but rather than suckle at its mother's teat, it rears up at once on warty leg and cloven hoof, and leers at the soul to which it has been assigned.

Now does eternity of pain commence, and the various crimes and misdemeanours of the victim are weighed and measured, and appropriate punishment devised.

So here are the fornicators, penetrated forever with pokers red-hot from the furnace.

And here are the thieves, writhing in agony on beds of

thorns as snakes bite and suck at their skin, their fingers, their eyes.

Those who lied, who inflicted the disease of untruth upon their fellow men, suffer from every disease that ever was known to man, and many that have not yet been known. Their skin falls from their bones, their eyes bleed, their hair falls from their skulls, and loud is their groaning, loud!

The corrupt are immersed in lakes of boiling tar.

The sorcerers have their heads twisted backwards.

The suicides are turned into trees and are pecked at by harpies.

The violent are piled upon each other in a pit that has no bottom, and arrows are fired at them should they try and climb thereout.

But, O Lord, is Hell only waiting for us after death, at the moment of judgement?

Or is it already here?

After giving The Word today, I made my rounds of the village and I saw these three things.

I saw Grimes the landlord weeping from the pain in his hands and his back as he heaves the barrels of beer into his cellar. His bones have weakened on him, his wife is frail and blind and can give no help, his son is dead in the war in America.

I saw a family of bodies sickening in a single cell in the

huts by the farm, for that is their whole space, each one infected with the illnesses of the other, each too hungry to move all the livelong day.

I saw the Meadows boy kicking at a cat, fetching it a great boot up the behind, and when I called him and bid him stop, and bid him tell me why it was he did this thing, he did not answer, but ran away. As he ran I saw upon his brow and his cheek the swellings of the bruises from his father's fist.

Hell is upon me.

Hell is upon us all, unseen, at every turn.

Lord, will you not save us yet?

Must we wait so long?

Must we wait in vain?

The day is done, and Rebecca suddenly wants not to be sitting under a damp bridge listening to ghost stories.

She gets up abruptly and leaves the secrecy of the arch, not bothering to ask if Ferelith is coming.

'Meet me tomorrow?' Ferelith asks.

Rebecca doesn't answer. Instead she asks a question of her own.

'So you never told me. Do you believe in God?'

Ferelith raises an eyebrow.

'Yes, I believe in God. But you know, the trouble is, I don't think He believes in me. Not really.'

Her voice is a strange mix. She's trying to be sardonic, but Rebecca senses something frail, almost vulnerable, underneath. Just a hint. But she can see she's not going to get a straight answer and stalks away through the tumbling vegetation of the grounds of the Hall.

'Two o'clock?' Ferelith calls after her.

She doesn't reply.

Suddenly she feels very alone, and fishes in her pocket for her mobile.

She calls Adam.

She's almost surprised when he answers.

'Yeah?'

'It's me,' she says, feeling defensive already. He doesn't say anything at first, so she goes on.

'How are you?'

'What do you want?'

His voice is cold. Her heart quickens.

'What do I want?' she asks, feeling anger rising inside. 'I thought I might speak to my boyfriend, that's all.'

'Listen, Becky.'

'What?' she says, then stops herself. She makes herself speak more gently. 'What?'

'Listen. The thing is, I'm not your boyfriend. Right?'

'You're . . . what? What do you . . . ?'

'Listen, just forget it, okay? I've got to go now, anyway.'

Then Rebecca hears laughter, but this time, it's just one other voice. A girl's voice. She hears the girl speak to Adam.

'Come on,' she says.

That's all. But Rebecca doesn't need to hear any more to know what's going on.

She hangs up, then immediately thumbs for the last dialled number. She hesitates, staring at the number. Inside her she feels the seeds of disbelief, panic, and pain. They grow.

She's still staring at the number as she gets back to The Street, and is surprised to see her father's car outside the house. She shoves her mobile back in her pocket.

Suddenly her father comes out of the house looking slightly ridiculous, wearing yellow rubber gloves and carrying a big bucket.

On the ground beside the car she sees an array of bottles, white spirit, kitchen cleaners, and a big sponge.

Her father is scrubbing away furiously at the side of the car and doesn't see her coming, but when he does, his face darkens and he doesn't say a word.

'Dad,' she says, 'What is it?'

He doesn't answer, just keeps on scrubbing at the mess on the side of the car.

Something is written there, in big red letters, bright against the white bodywork.

It's hard to read because someone, presumably her father, has tried to clean it off, and now he's making even more of a mess of it with whatever cleaning fluids he can get his hands on.

But she can read enough of it to know what it says.

'Who did it?' she asks quietly, but still he says nothing.

He throws the sponge he's using into the bucket, stands and kicks the side of the car.

Three old ladies are walking by, staring at her, at the mess, at her father standing there with washing-up gloves on. They whisper something to each other and

Rebecca glares till they move on.

He kicks the side of the car again.

'Dad, don't,' Rebecca says, but her father is not listening.

More people are passing and looking and her father turns and strides into the house, slamming the door.

Rebecca is left in the road, without the beginning of an idea of what to do.

She gazes at the side of the car.

He's barely managed to remove any of the paint, and it's still possible to make out what someone has scrawled across it in tall red letters.

CHILD KILLER.

Today I read the Apocalypse.

As I have read it so many times before. Is it really so that there is a false Church, a Church of falsehoods, ruled by the Lord of Lies? And is it so that this anti-Church is the object of God's wrath and that it shall be destroyed at the day of judgement?

And if it is, then why must we wait till doomsday?

Why must we wait for evil to be vanquished?

1798, 9m, 24d.

Ate and drank, but to live, and no more. I am indeed a virtuous and devout fellow.

Rose early to prayer, and bowed long and low before the Lord.

1798, 9m, 26d.

Displayed a notable tenderness of being today, and thought me of the trumpet of God sounding to eternity.

O Lord. Again my wretched dwarfish self emerges like a very demon and betrays me. Last night I sinned, of the flesh. I am going straight to Hell.

And yet though all is prepared with the good doctor Barrieux, I am hesitant to commence our great and noble work.

I went to the Hall today and made it my purpose to speak to him upon this issue, and to question him for the thousandth time about our intentions, but when I came hence, I found that he had turned each of my arguments aside with ease, and that I found my purpose and vigour for the project renewed.

The Lord wrote ten Commandments on tablets of stone. We will break three of them, for the least, I am sure. And yet I find I do not heed this sin, such is the power of the doctor's argument.

The Hall was quiet. All the workmen gone unseen in the night, just as they had arrived.

There was nothing left to do but to commence our labours and yet there remains one unanswered conundrum, one puzzle that we must solve before we can begin.

How are we to find souls for this undertaking of ours?

Kindertotenlieder

Of course, no one thinks he actually killed the girl. Well, no one sane, anyway. But how did the report put it? *'Severe negligence on the part of Detective Inspector John Case that can only have contributed to the girl's death.'*

The girl. No one even knows her name, not while it's still under appeal. Of course all the newspapers and the TV people know, but until he's had his chance to appeal they have to keep quiet about it.

Becky's father doesn't have that anonymity though, and now everyone knows who he is and why he's 'after a quieter life' in the countryside.

Poor Becky.

She and her dad didn't come out for days after that thing with the car. They ordered lots of pizza and a van came with food from the supermarket, or that's what they said in the pub, anyway.

Must be tough living with something like that hanging over you. But not as tough as being the parents of the dead girl, I guess.

You wonder how someone copes with that. I suppose if you believe in these things, you can think, little Tracey, or whatever her name is, little Tracey's in Heaven now. And that must make you feel better.

But supposing little Tracey was an absolute pig. I know it's not nice to speak ill of the dead, but it's possible, for the sake of argument, that even though she was only fifteen that she was a violent, thieving, lying, nasty piece of work. And in that case, has little Tracey gone to Heaven, or is she down below, toasting slowly on a big pitchfork while the Devil and some of his mates laugh about it all?

But anyway, assuming little Tracey was an angel on earth, then she's an angel now, floating on a cloud somewhere I suppose, or riding an invisible pony, and it must make her parents feel better to think that. Better to think that than to think she's gone forever, and they can remember her, and think of her and sing songs for her. Songs for dead children.

And if that's where she is, then there's even the chance that she might contact her parents, with a sign, or a haunting, or a visitation. Or even a postcard. I don't know, but all I'm saying, is that if she did, then she'd be the white crow.

And it only takes one.

The week passes like an agony for Rebecca. A slow and painful torment. Her father has shut down, barely speaks to her, drags himself out of bed and out of the door, drags himself back home again.

He stares at the TV every evening, a fast food box or a ready meal on his lap, and a can of beer in his hand. It's as though he's switched off, just like that, like a light going out. Suddenly, Rebecca realises, he's not there for her any more.

For the first time, as she understands this, she understands too that maybe it's not all his fault. That maybe she's let her father down too, treating him as if he's as guilty as they say he is.

She feels desperate, switching between pity and anger on an hourly basis. Then she thinks about calling *him*, not even bringing herself to think his name for fear of it hurting too much. Then she realises how stupid it is to want to call someone who she can't even bear to think of, but though she knows it's stupid, and that it hurts, she brings Adam's number up on her phone, and stares at it, feeling it, as though she's twisting the knife a bit more, wondering how much it can possibly hurt.

She stares at her phone, her thumb hovering over the call button, and somehow she manages to talk herself out of it every time.

She stares at the ceiling of her bedroom, she stares out of her window at the sea, at the beautiful scenery and the sunshine which should make her feel happy to be alive, but which only reinforces how miserable she is. She's kept Adam's crucifix round her neck, but now something snaps in her and almost without looking at it she takes it off. Her hand hovers over the wastebin, but in the end she drops it into her dressing table drawer.

As she does, she sees her jewellery box, and lifts it out. Feeling very young and with a tinge of sadness, she feels something inside the box almost call out to her. She opens it, lifts her father's heart pendant out, and holds it in her hand for a long time, wondering whether to put it back on again, and what it will mean if she does. If anything.

The next day, she finds herself standing at the bar of The Angel and The Devil at eleven o'clock in the morning, speaking to a man who must be the landlord of the pub.

'Yes, Miss?' he asks, friendly enough, though there's the slight mistrust in his eyes that everyone seems to wear in Winterfold. He keeps on wiping glasses with a ragged tea towel as he speaks to her.

'I just wanted to know something,' Rebecca says, and shifts her weight from one foot to the other, 'and I thought you might know. In here.'

She looks around, even hoping to speak to the dreadful Melanie rather than this old guy.

'Well?'

'Well,' Rebecca says, 'I was wondering if you know where Ferelith lives. Do you know Ferelith? The girl I was here with the other day. I know she lives in Long Lane, but...'

'Yes,' the landlord says. His voice has changed. 'Yes, I know where Ferelith lives. Why do you want to know?'

'I just wanted to visit her. That's all.'

113

The landlord considers this for long time. He stops wiping glasses, and puts the tea towel down on the bar. He leans towards her.

'She lives in the Old Rectory,' he says at last, 'but I wouldn't go there if I were you.'

Rebecca feels a bit weirded out all of a sudden, as if she's in some cheesy Vampire movie.

'Thanks for the advice,' she says, turning to go.

'Your funeral,' the landlord adds as she goes.

Give me a break, thinks Rebecca, now having the distinct feeling that she's heading off to visit Dracula's castle. She's had the warning from the spooky innkeeper, now all she needs is a black coach and four to stop by and pick her up.

She even looks up The Street waiting for the clip-clopping of hooves on the tarmac.

'Thank Goodness I have my father's love to protect me,' she jokes to herself, fingering the little silver heart at her neck.

It's ironic, she thinks. The crucifix that Adam gave her would have been better protection against vampires.

She finds The Old Rectory easily enough, and is surprised. It's the big house with the high wall that she heard the loud music coming from on her first trip round the village.

She stands at the entrance to the drive, a pair of

large iron gates stuck permanently open, overgrown by bindweed and ground elder. The gravel drive is a lovely, sweeping semi circle, but like everything else about the place it could do with some attention.

The house itself is big, very big, with a crazy mix of architecture, pointed Victorian gables on the front, giving way to an older stone building at the back.

Once again feeling as if she's in a lite-bite movie, she hesitates at the threshold of Ferelith's world. Maybe she's not in, maybe she's busy, maybe she's got friends, maybe she doesn't want Rebecca to call anyway.

'What's the worst that can happen?' Rebecca says out loud and, feeling nervous, though without knowing why, she crunches across the weed strewn gravel and gives the doorbell a long push.

Nothing happens for a while, but she can hear sounds inside, so she tries again and eventually the door opens.

It's not Ferelith, but a young guy, maybe twenty-something. The first thing Rebecca notices is that he smells. His hair is long, dreads reach down his back. He's unshaven and dressed as if he's going to work in the garden, even though he clearly isn't. He's just woken up.

He stands and stares at Rebecca, and straightens his back; she tends to have that effect on most males.

'Er . . . Hi. Is Ferelith in?' she asks.

The young man nods, and turns, heading off into the gloom. Inside the house it's surprisingly dark given the bright sunlight outside.

'Where is she?' Rebecca calls after the disappearing figure.

'In her room.'

'Which is?' she says, starting to feel a little frustrated.

He points up the stairs.

'Keep right, head to the back of the house. Big black door.'

He goes into the kitchen, the door of which swings shut behind him, and Rebecca's left alone in the hall.

She looks about, and can't quite work out what's going on. She's never been in an English country rectory before. There's an old umbrella stand by the front door, with three battered umbrellas in it; there's a mirrored hall table, and various old paintings of quaint rural scenes. But then there are other unexpected paintings, disturbing abstracts and even more disturbing figures. Bodies.

And there's the sound of music coming from somewhere upstairs, but it's not Chopin or Brahms, it's some weird noise with shifting beats and detuned guitars.

And rather than burnt toast and marmalade coming from the kitchen, it's the smell of dope.

Rebecca heads upstairs, and follows the directions the hippy guy gave her.

In front of her is a big black door, just as he said.

116

From behind it comes more music, which again Rebecca can't place.

She approaches, and knocks on the door, twice, hard.

It opens, and Ferelith is standing there. Somehow Rebecca is not surprised that Ferelith can even do goth in her sleep-wear, but she can. She's wearing loose dark grey cotton shorts down to her knees, and a baggy black T-shirt. She looks deadly somehow.

For a second Rebecca thinks she might be angry, but then realises that she's just thrown.

Ferelith smiles.

'So,' she says, resting her weight on one hip. 'You came.'

1798, 10m, 3d.

It was Dr Barrieux himself who solved the problem.

At last, he had come to dine with me, having kept himself to the Hall for the duration of our labours.

Our views differ greatly. In fact, aside from the single fact that we share the same objective, our views on what is meant by every term we use could not be more different.

If I say, – Hell, then the doctor says to me, – describe Hell! And when I do, he merely laughs.

And if I mention the celestial realm of our wonderful Lord, he laughs twice as hard.

And yet, when I say, – Doctor, so tell me, where are your daughter and your wife now? Where are they? Tell me! Where are they? He falls silent and will not work for the rest of the day.

We each have our demons, but whatever they may be, there still remained the problem to solve, and so we turned our talk to that end.

We need souls. In short, we need people, and we were both at a loss as to how to tempt them to cross the threshold.

The only thought we clung to was that the participants

must come willingly to the Hall, not through threat, or through coercion, or bribery.

And then, as we drained another jug of wine, Dr Barrieux suddenly sat bolt upright.

- Hear me now! He said.

And he expounded his scheme, and I bethought it subtle in its design and powerful in its simplicity.

He outlined the message that we would put out to the world, and wait for the world to come to us, and I saw the power of what he said, for the thing that we would offer the world would be the very thing that we ourselves craved.

The knowledge.

The truth.

The answer, to what lies beyond.

And now, there only remained one obstacle; how should we send this message, how should it become known what we were offering?

And at that moment, Martha entered the room to clear our plates, and to bring us more wine.

The doctor smiled at Martha, who, bless her modesty, attended her gaze only to the top of the table, and so she did not see as the doctor smiled at me instead and then returned his gaze to the innocent woman.

Yes, I thought.

Yes.

That is the way.

Ferelith and Rebecca sit on the floor of Ferelith's bedroom, on a big Turkish rug that's seen better days. Ferelith has turned the music down but it still chunters on quietly from some unseen speakers.

'Your room is amazing,' Rebecca says, quite honestly. She's not jealous of it, because it's not how she would ever like her room to be, but amazing it is.

It's full of stuff. Every square inch of floor, wall, and in some places ceiling has something on it. Every bookcase, and there are many, is crammed to overflowing, not just with books, piled in sideways where there's no room, but with all manner of things: interesting stones from the beach, bone-dry sticks, bleached by sun and saltwater, smooth green sea glass. There's a bunch of dried mistletoe, rusty scissors that will cut nothing again. A jar of feathers, all of them black, save one that is white.

There are two big wardrobes, and the door of one of them is open, showing a mirror and a rail full of what Rebecca can only think of as 'Ferelith clothes', mostly black, some muted colours, all very simple, all quite sexy in an unusual way.

'You want a drink or something?' Ferelith asks, but she doesn't really seem to be offering, so Rebecca shakes her head.

'So, you're kind of famous, then,' Ferelith says, changing the subject.

Rebecca bristles.

'Don't be stupid.'

'Do the press know your dad is here? I bet they do. They know everything. I guess there's just something else to write about for now. I remember it though. It was last year, wasn't it?'

Rebecca is about to correct her, but decides she doesn't want to talk about it.

'I came here so I wouldn't have to think about it, all right?' she snaps angrily.

Ferelith sits back. She doesn't say anything for a very long time, waiting for Rebecca's anger to pass.

'God. You are so beautiful,' Ferelith says eventually.

'Shut up,' says Rebecca, but she's speaking gently. She frowns. 'Do you like me?' Her nose wrinkles. 'Or something?'

'You mean, like I . . . Why? Would you like me to?'

'Of course not.'

'Then why do you ask?'

'Because of the things you say.'

'But you are beautiful.'

'I told you to shut up.'

'Fair enough. Do you like me, though?' She turns away, hiding her eyes behind a curtain of hair. Then adds in a small voice, 'Would it kill you to tell me I'm not ugly?'

Rebecca considers this. Ferelith is not beautiful. She is not pretty. Nor can she apply the words gorgeous, or stunning, or even handsome to her. But she's certainly not ugly. And there's something powerful about her, something powerfully attractive.

'Do you think you are?'

Ferelith shrugs, still turned away.

'They all said I was at school.'

'Kids say anything if they think it will hurt.'

Ferelith nods.

'Yeah. Why is that? Why do kids say things far worse than adults?'

'Trust me, adults can say bad stuff too.'

'Like what was on your car?' Ferelith asks, looking back at Rebecca now. She holds up her hand. 'Sorry. We don't have to talk about it, even if everyone else in the village is. It must be really hard.'

Rebecca says nothing. Then her face crumples and she folds into a small ball on the rug, and cries her heart out.

Ferelith watches her, thinking, waiting, thinking some more. Then she crawls over to Rebecca and puts a hand on her shoulder, then strokes her hair with her other one.

Rebecca whimpers like a wounded dog, and Ferelith pulls her into her arms and holds her tightly.

'Poor Becky,' she says, but Rebecca just rocks back and forth, sobbing quietly.

Eventually, the tears stop, and Ferelith finds a box of tissues for her. She blows her nose and wipes her face, and then Rebecca speaks again.

'You want to know the worst thing?'

Ferelith nods, not daring to speak, in case she breaks the spell.

'The worst thing. Worse than all the things kids said to me at school, worse than the newspaper people on our doorstep, worse than the things they said on the TV. The worst thing is that I look at my dad, and I don't know.

'I don't know what I think. I don't know whether he did something he shouldn't have. I don't know whether he's responsible for that girl dying. Or not. That's the worst thing.'

Cry Me a River

I spent a long time with Rebecca that day. In fact, it was late by the time she went home, back down Long Lane in the dark.

She seemed better after she'd cried, but that's often the way. Something to do with endorphins. Or serotonin, or some other chemical the body releases to make you feel better. Seems a shame that the stupid body can't release some of the same bloody chemicals and stop you from crying in the first place.

That's what I would have done if I was designing the body. But I didn't, God did. And if he didn't, then it was Charles Darwin who did. If you see what I mean.

But even then, some things don't make sense. Like, why do we cry? I mean, I can understand the physical need to cry if you get some grit in your eye. It washes it out, stops the grit from damaging your precious organs of sight.

But apart from that, why do we cry?

When we see a sad film, when Kevin says that he doesn't love you any more because Julie's not as fat as you are, when your hamster dies. Or when your mum goes crazy and your dad leaves you, why do we cry?

What's the point?

From evolution's point of view, I mean?

So anyway, we talked for a long time that afternoon, and I found some pizzas in the freezer that were mine and that no one else in the house had stolen, and we ate them, and I found a bottle of wine in Matthew's room that he won't miss because he's too stoned most of the time to know what's going on.

Rebecca said she didn't want to drink, but I told her it was medicinal, and that was all it took for her to slug back half a bottle in half an hour.

Then we dozed in the sun coming in from the big window over the garden, until we watched it set behind the firs at the end of the garden and the room grew dark, and as it grew dark, all Rebecca's pain and all my pain grew darker and softer too, and a gentle tired ease entered my body and my mind.

I felt really happy, but just as I was thinking that, Rebecca spoke, for the first time in hours.

'Christ,' she said. 'I feel so bloody, bloody, bloody lonely.'

I sat up.

'But you've got me, now,' I said.

And then she sat up too.

She looked deeply at me.

'Have I?' she said, like it was a surprise.

'Yes,' I said, 'of course you have. For better or worse.'

And she smiled.

126

1798, 10m, 4ᵭ.

What are the tools of the angels?

The tools of the angels are light, sunlight, golden sunlight. The light illuminates us and displays the truth, God's truth, and this leads us to the path of righteousness, and the path of righteousness leads us to Heaven.

These are the tools of the angels.

What are the tools of the Devil?

The tools of the Devil are shadow, illusion, and darkness. With these tools he obscures the truth, and casts false images to rise before us, and hides the path to righteousness. In its stead we are led down the path of evil, and the path of evil leads us to Hell.

These are the tools of the Devil.

Rebecca becomes a regular visitor to the Rectory, as the two girls spend more and more time with each other.

One day, Rebecca suddenly realises that life has got easier, despite everything. She's stopped looking at her mobile every ten minutes, hoping there'll be a text, a missed call.

Despite her father's problems, nothing more has happened since the business with the car, and although it's unspoken, they both wonder whether whoever did it, person, or persons unknown, realises they've overstepped the mark and have backed off.

John Case has noticed that his daughter is wearing that heart pendant again, and it helps him, though he knows better than to mention the fact.

Maybe they can settle down for the rest of the summer until it's time for her to go back to London, time for her father's appeal. And she'll have to face Adam, too, when school starts again. Suddenly Winterfold seems like an attractive option.

The weather burns fiercely, day after day. There's been no rain for almost two months, and the land is scorched and dry. Everyone moves slowly, drags themselves about in the heat, and the days are long and light, making it seem as if time itself has slowed.

But it's always cool in the darkness of the Rectory.

On Saturday the seventh of August, Rebecca and Ferelith are in the room with the black door, listening to music, talking when one of them feels like it, saying nothing when they don't.

They have one earphone each, and so close, Rebecca watches Ferelith mouthing the words to the song.

'. . . If you fall, I will catch you. I'll be waiting. Time after time.'

Rebecca wonders what it is she's seeing on Ferelith's face, and then places it. It's happiness.

Ferelith sits up suddenly.

'I never showed you, did I?' she says.

'Showed me what?' Rebecca asks.

'My collection. It's in the trunk. Do you want to see? Say you do!'

'Your collection of what?'

'Of stuff I've found on the beach. From graves.'

Rebecca wrinkles her nose.

'Are you scared or something?' Ferelith asks.

'No,' Rebecca says, automatically, but actually, she's not scared. It's something else she can't put her finger on.

'So do you want to see, or not?' Ferelith asks, but she's already clearing all the mess off the top of the old pine blanket box by the window, and is lifting the lid.

'Go on then,' Rebecca says, aware she's not being given a choice.

'Look!' Ferelith says, her eyes gleaming, 'Treasure!'

She pulls out an old pocket watch, battered and broken. The face is missing, but it's obviously silver.

'You found that on the beach?' Rebecca asks.

'The night after a storm. About three years ago, when St James's churchyard was going over. A whole lot of graves went in the course of the winter. I got some great things.'

'But that's stealing.'

'Only if you get caught,' Ferelith says, grinning. 'But who am I stealing from anyway? Someone would have to own this stuff for it to be stealing, wouldn't they?'

Does a crime have to have a victim for it to be a crime? Rebecca thinks.

'So what else have you got in there?'

'Look at this,' Ferelith says. 'I could only find the left one.'

It's a leather boot, a ladies leather boot. Obviously once something quite fine for a rich lady, though now rotten and spoiled.

'Take it,' Ferelith says, handing the boot to Rebecca, who takes it gingerly and pretends to inspect it.

'Amazing,' she says, though her voice is flat.

'Okay then. Let's see if you're more impressed by this.'

Ferelith rummages deep in the trunk, her back to Rebecca, and then she suddenly turns round and waves a skull in her face. A human skull.

Rebecca shrieks. She recoils from the skull, rocking back on her heels. 'Are you trying to scare me?'

'Only a little bit,' Ferelith says, laughing. 'Isn't it cool? It's the only one I've found and I guess it must be three hundred years old or so. That's the age of the graves that were going in at the time. I found it on a freezing morning, and smuggled it home. There were some people walking dogs along the beach and they'd have sniffed it out if I'd been five minutes later. Isn't it cool?'

Rebecca's thinking.

'Do you want to touch it? Go on, touch it.'

Ferelith holds it out again, urging Rebecca to do as she says.

'No, I don't want to.'

'It's okay if you're scared.'

'I'm not scared,' Rebecca says. And she isn't. She's realised what she finds uncomfortable. 'It's just that it's all about death, isn't it? About death. You know?'

Ferelith nods.

'I know. But that's all I'm asking. Are you scared of

131

death? Are you scared of dying?'

'No,' Rebecca says. 'I'm not. No.'

But she's lying, and they both know it.

1798, 10m, 6ð.

I was genius today.

I acted exactly as the doctor had advised me, and though I pride myself, I hold that I played the part required as an actor on any stage in London or Paris.

– Martha.

– Yes, Sir, what is't?

– Martha, I am sore worried.

– Why so, Sir?

Bless her that she is a good and careful servant, and attends to me with great diligence.

– You will recall that I entertained the newly come doctor but three days past.

– Indeed so, Sir. I'm sorry, Sir. Was the beef not good?

– The beef was excellent, thank you, Martha. No, it is the doctor who concerns me. You retired, as the hour grew late, but the doctor stayed awhile longer and yet we did speak.

– Sir?

My voice I made to grow quiet at this.

133

- Indeed. And what the doctor spoke of has vexed me ever since... I believe he plans some great mischief at the Hall. I believe he intends to practice some unholy rite, a summoning, a conjuration. A thing of magic.

Martha stared at me, lost in confusion.

I hit upon another approach which I then ventured.

- Tell me. Do you believe in Heaven?

- Oh, yes, Sir, she cried.

- Good. And do you, therefore, believe in Hell?

At this she began to shake.

- Indeed, Sir.

She crossed herself.

- And for which place, Martha, are you headed? Do you know?

She shook her head.

- I do not.

- But Martha. That is precisely what the doctor intends to discover, for any person so wishing to know. Would you not like to know such a thing?

She shook her head.

- Indeed not, Sir.

- Quite right. It is an evil undertaking and will lead only to pain and suffering, and blasphemy. That is so, and you are goodly and wise to see it. But you see, Martha, I fear greatly that others, other people, will not have your good sense.

- Indeed, Sir?

- Indeed, I said. Now, it is Sunday afternoon, and your leisure hours are at hand. Enjoy yourself, and think no more on what I have said. It is an evil business and not one to be concerned upon.

- Very good, Sir.

She left, and I watched her go down Long Lane, and I knew full well that the doctor was right.

She would go straight to The Angel, the local tavern, and I knew just what she would talk about once she came there.

The doctor is wise in the ways of the world.

This is How I Disappear

We sat in the Lover's Seat and fried.

The sun was beating down just as it had been for days and days.

'So what's with your boyfriend then?' I asked Rebecca. She seemed needled.

'He's not my boyfriend any more.'

I nodded.

She stared out to sea. Then she turned back to me.

'So what's with your mother then?' she asked.

I changed the subject.

'How about an ice-cream?' I said.

'You're always asking me questions. I want to ask you one. What's with your mother?'

I got cross. I shouted and told her to mind her own business.

I stomped about a bit, and it got even hotter. I stared down over the cliff edge at the hard beach and the blue water, and after a while I stopped being angry.

'I'd love an ice-cream,' Rebecca said then. 'But I don't have any money.'

I fished around in my pockets and found nothing useful.

'Never mind,' I said, 'I know where we can get some.'

'What does that mean?' she said,

I didn't answer, but put out my hands to pull her up.

'Come on,' I said, and lead the way, twisting down a little track to rejoin the main footpath.

I took a branch of that and we were walking down the lane that leads to the Hall. It's a very pretty lane with cottages dotted here and there like you see on cheap boxes of toffee.

And there was one cottage I was interested in especially.

At Rose Cottage there's usually a table outside in the summer where they sell things from their garden.

It was there, with some jars of jam and bundles of runner beans.

I stood by the table, and Rebecca joined me.

'Vegetables?' she said, but that wasn't what I was interested in. On the table next to the stuff was an old coffee jar with a slot in the lid to put the money.

An honesty box.

I looked through the front windows of the cottage. No one was visible.

'Check the lane for me,' I told Rebecca.

'What?' she said.

'Just check the lane. Is it clear?'

'Yes, but...'

Before she'd finished I swiped the tin and stuck it under my T-shirt.

137

She stood looking stupid by the table.

'Come on,' I hissed.

'You…' she said. It was kind of funny. 'You can't do that.'

But I was halfway down the lane and she was still at the table. I picked up speed and Rebecca began to follow me at last.

As she did, some little old dear came out of the cottage.

'Can I help you?' she asked Rebecca, who was left stranded.

She must have mumbled something to the old girl and then she walked away, trying to catch up with me, but I was out of sight and running then, and I didn't stop till I was outside the shop, clutching just enough money for two big ice creams.

1798, 10m, 22d.

It has started.

More than one of my parishioners has whispered to me that they have heard this and this, or such and such, and I have simply shaken my head and explained that just because Dr Barrieux is French does not mean he is the Devil! Or that he consorts with the same.

Nevertheless, today, Dr Barrieux sent a sealed note to me by way of a village boy, and the message was a short one.

– We have a beginning.

So, someone is prepared to try their luck in the Candle Room, and we shall soon see what we shall see.

John Case blusters round the house like a storm with nowhere to go.

'I know it's hard here,' he says. 'It's hard for both of us. But do you really have to go and make it worse?'

Rebecca sits at the kitchen table, arms folded, staring into space while she gets the lecture.

'This is just the sort of place where you put a foot wrong and they have you.'

'It wasn't me,' Rebecca says again.

'Becky, you were seen. The tin was gone and you were seen by Mrs Trentham.'

Something stops Rebecca from putting the blame on Ferelith.

'Do you have any idea what it felt like to get this message from the station that "the new girl in the village" had stolen someone's honesty box? My own daughter! Can't you think? I won't even tell you the things they were saying.'

He slams his fist on the table and Rebecca jumps.

She turns on him.

'And do you have any idea what it's like being your

140

daughter right now? Don't tell me you have a clue because you don't.'

The air is torn by their pain as they fight, pain made all the worse by the love between them, a love lying wounded in the corner of the room.

Eventually her father runs out of steam, and all he can think is one final thing.

'It was that girl, wasn't it? Ferelith?'

'Dad . . .'

'I know it was. I know you wouldn't do something like this.'

'How do you know anything I'd do? When did you last talk to me? When did you last ask how I am? You have no idea what's going on in my head, or what I would or wouldn't do.'

And with that, she gets up, grabs her phone and storms her way out of the front door.

She texts.

You about?

And she gets one straight back.

Yeah. You fancy breaking the law?

141

Dead of Night

The great thing about trespassing is that it's free. And anything in life that makes you feel good is worth doing, so if it's free too, it only makes it better.

Rebecca told me about the thing with her dad, and she told me that she hadn't told him it was me.

'Thanks,' I said, smiling.

She frowned.

'I've never done this before, but it's stupid, isn't it?,' she said. 'I mean, it's what kids do, isn't it?'

I sighed.

'Trust me,' I said. 'You never grow out of this. It's great.'

And it was.

We started in the village.

From the Rectory you can hop over the wall into four different gardens.

It was dusk as we set off and I knew we wouldn't be seen from anyone's house, if they had the light on inside.

Rebecca hesitated for ages and I had to kind of convince her to do it, but she ran fast once she'd started and I had a job to keep up.

We dropped off the Rectory wall and into the rose

beds at the bottom of the Symons' place. Their house is big, almost out of sight from where we were, but Rebecca panicked anyway, and was off across the grass to a spot I'd pointed out behind their summerhouse.

I caught up with her and she was panting madly, but she's pretty fit and I knew it wasn't from the running.

She stared at me and then began laughing.

'Wow!' she whispered. 'Why is that such fun?'

I grinned. I could see she felt it. The same thing I felt. The thrill of it, the danger of being caught, the exhilaration of getting away with it.

'Don't know, but it is. Let's up the stakes a bit.'

'How?'

'Dares.'

'Dares? Like the swimming thing? That really is for kids.'

But I knew I had her this time, because before I said anything else, she pointed to a fountain in the middle of the Dobsons' lawn.

'You,' she said. 'There and back. And I want wet hands to prove it.'

It was easy, and I was back before she knew it.

'Right,' I said. 'Your turn. Come on. Next garden.'

'Wait. What's the penalty? If you don't do a dare?'

'Total forfeit. You have to do the very next thing the other one says.'

She laughed.

'Anything?'

'Absolutely anything.'

We were over their fence in a moment and I pointed to the conservatory on the back of the next house.

'There! And bang on the glass.'

'But there's lights on.'

'So? That's not how this works. Be harder for them to see you anyway.'

She looked nervous.

'Are you going to lose already?' I said, and with that she was off across the dewy evening grass.

As she got to the house, she slipped and banged into the glass of the conservatory hard.

She scrambled up and fled back to where I was ducking out of sight behind a shed.

She swore.

'Shh! Someone's there.'

The door to the conservatory opened and someone called out. Just once. Then went in again.

'They probably think it was a bird,' I said.

Rebecca turned to me.

'Your turn. Only . . . This isn't fair, I don't know as many places as you do.'

'So. You should have though of that before you started.'

'All right,' she said. 'You have to go and knock on the front door of the next house.'

'Is that all?' I said.

'No,' she said. 'You have to stay there and when they

answer the door, you have to say you've lost your cat . . .'

'But everyone round here knows me. They know I don't have a cat.'

'You should have thought of that,' she said, 'And you have to say these exact words. "I've lost my pussy and it's called Mitzi. Please will you tell me if you find Mitzi."'

She was getting the hang of a difficult dare and I did what she asked, but I thought I needed to take control before she came up with something really imaginative.

'So,' I said, leaving some bewildered villager promising to look out for Mitzi. 'Your turn. And I think it's time we changed the venue. Come on.'

'Where are we going?'

'Come on,' I said.

She followed but she wouldn't let it drop.

'Ferelith. Where are we going?'

I stopped and looked at her. The dusk was complete and the night drawing in fast. It was perfect. Everything was perfect, and everything was ready.

I smiled.

'We're going to the graveyard.'

1798, 10m, 24d.

I have been woeful and suffered greatly these past days. Demons have come to me as I lay in my cot and tormented me with many thoughts and visions which should not be any person's to see. And yet I have seen them, and have had to bear the full terror of the message they bring.

The terrors of the night are easy to summon, and hard to dispel, and as yet we have not even begun our own explorations into these occult realms. These voyages of science, as the doctor prefers to call it, I know to be unholy blasphemies, and yet pursue them we must.

We must.

And that time is near at hand now, for the first of them arrives tonight.

I wonder what will happen.

Will the answers be revealed to us tonight?

Or will we learn maybe at least some small secret, which may be as a foundation stone to the work we do?

Or will we have the doors of perception slammed shut in our face, barring all, and permitting no knowledge at all?

As I write, my pen shakes.

What are we doing?

What are we doing?

Truly, will the angels lead us in God's way? Or is this the Devil's work?

1798, 10m, 25d.

Nothing.

A false start.

I had made my way by the cover of the night to the Hall, and together the doctor and I waited for the sound of the bell, but none came.

We had expected a certain woman, not of this parish in fact, but of our neighbour's, which does but show that our message has already been widely sent. We had expected this lady, by way of rumours reaching us through the boy the doctor uses to contact those outside the Hall.

But she did not come.

We waited all night.

I slept ill on a cramped couch in the study.

I go to my bed now, though the sun is high to noon.

What is it that I find to be so obstinate in the depiction of Heaven?

I can paint paintings in my head of Hell. I think I can truly say, I know what occurs there. I can conceive of it, and I can see that it is a thing of logic. How it works, the way it is, how it is. Punishments for sins. The pain. The eternity of pain.

The fact remains that I am unable to do the same for Heaven. What is Heaven like? Nothing I can think makes any sense. Nothing seems real, to have a place in the reality of my thoughts. To be believable. To exist.

Is Heaven somewhere in the sky, with the clouds? Or is God so great that perhaps Heaven exists in some way that we do not understand, that we cannot understand. In some place that is not of this world.

The same cannot be said of Hell. I know where Hell is.

It is underground, it is beneath our feet. It is in the earth, down, down, in the direction that the doctor has dug under the Hall, but further. Yes, further, I pray.

And if I know where Hell is, and what it looks like, and what occurs there, and if I cannot know the same for

Heaven, then what does this signify?

A monstrous thought assails me!

Does this pertain because the one place exists and the other does not?

How terrible would that be!

That only Hell exists.

1798, 10m, 26ð.

Perhaps our time is at an end now, our time of impatience, for rumour has reached us of another volunteer.

A man in the village is near to death with some ailment, I know not what.

I care not. So long as he succumbs, his illness will have served a purpose.

He wishes to know what lies beyond, what lies in wait for him. And through him, we may learn what lies in wait for us all, when our own time is come.

Praise be to God.

Ferelith refuses to answer any more of Rebecca's questions as they tread the silent night summer-scented path to the churchyard.

Wafts of honeysuckle and dog rose hang over their journey, and it is a warm and close evening, as if the air is desperate for rainfall that will not come. The path is dry and dusty underfoot, and Rebecca watches Ferelith's slight and elfin form ahead of her, merely a silhouette, bobbing and weaving.

She wonders about the odd girl she has met, and though she feels very close to her now, she realises with quick shock that she actually knows very little about her.

She knows where she lives, but not really who with. She doesn't know who owns the house where she lives, she doesn't know how she gets any money to live on. A thought flashes through her mind that perhaps she's a drug dealer; she could go into town once a month and sell enough to live on comfortably. Rebecca's dad is always saying that this stretch of the coast is rife with drug-drops, and smuggling, as if this is the eighteenth century, not the twenty-first.

She dismisses the thought. Wouldn't she have tried to have pushed some on her by now, if that were the case?

She knows very little too about Ferelith's parents. Her father leaving. Her mother going crazy. That must have a pretty bad affect on anyone, especially at the age of fourteen. She doesn't know if there are any brothers or sisters, she only knows that she is so intelligent that she finished school years earlier than normal people.

There's another word she catches herself using. Normal.

And is it intelligent to be so very able with facts and knowledge at that age, or is it actually a bit weird?

They're nearly at the churchyard of St Mary's.

'Where are we going?' Rebecca asks.

'I told you.'

Rebecca knows but she wants a better explanation. She tries another tack, forcing some lightness into her voice.

'So, what's my dare then?'

Ferelith doesn't even answer that.

'This isn't funny,' Rebecca shouts, suddenly losing her temper.

'Hey. Cool it. We're there. You'll see.'

Rebecca sighs, and follows her round beyond the perfect front of the church, looking through the dark at the great front door that Ferelith opened to reveal her temple to the sea. It already seems a long time since that night.

She thinks about her father, chasing his own daughter round a shadowy churchyard, but pushes the thought away.

The sounds of the sea come clearly in the still night air, the rushing of the waves on the beach below the cliff sailing up to them like the soundtrack from a dark but gentle dream.

Ferelith takes Rebecca by the hand.

'Close your eyes,' she says. But Rebecca doesn't. Not at first.

She's still angry.

It's gone midnight and suddenly she feels very tired and cold. But Ferelith insists.

'You have to do your dare,' she says. 'Shut your eyes.'

'All right then. But if it isn't over in ten minutes I'm going home.'

She shuts her eyes and though the churchyard was pitch black anyway, now she can see nothing at all.

It's an unsettling feeling she thinks, being led, blind. It requires a great deal of trust, and she realises that she doesn't trust Ferelith enough.

She's about to say so when they come to a stop.

'Open your eyes,' Ferelith says.

When Rebecca does she doesn't get it at first. It's so dark now, and although her eyes have adjusted to night vision she can see absolutely nothing.

'What?' she says, feeling irritable.

'There,' says Ferelith. 'Your dare. It's right in front of you!'

Rebecca looks, looks right down at her feet.

She can vaguely sense something now, a greater darkness in the gloom that surrounds them.

'Is that what I think it is?'

'Uh-huh,' Ferelith says. 'And all you have to do is lie down in it.'

'No way.'

'That's your dare.'

'What's it even doing here?'

Now she knows what it is, somehow Rebecca can see it more easily. A grave. An open, unused grave, only partially dug, with the spoil from the digging piled to one side, covered in weeds.

'It was being dug at the time the church wall collapsed. For someone from the village, I guess. They never filled it up again. It's been here for years.'

'I'm not doing it.'

'It's your dare. That, or the forfeit.'

Rebecca says nothing.

'Your choice.'

She thinks.

'For how long?'

'As long as you want. But you have to lie down in it properly.'

'Okay. But if I ruin these jeans you can buy me new ones.'

'Okay. Deal.'

Rebecca crouches, and then slowly sits down, her feet hanging into the empty space. In reality the grave is not so deep, and she can feel the bottom with her toes.

She's about to lower herself in, when Ferelith speaks again.

'Oh,' she says, 'There's one other thing. You ought to see whose grave it is, first.'

'What do you mean?'

And from nowhere Ferelith pulls out a torch, flicking it on and shining it at the head of the grave. The beam plays on something pale there and for a moment Rebecca is blinded.

She blinks and then she sees what Ferelith is showing her.

A gravestone.

A gravestone with a name on it, and a date, and an inscription.

It reads, In Loving Memory. She Departs This World.

The date is 13th August 2010.

The name is Rebecca Case.

She swears and then swears some more, and drags

herself out of the gravehole, the Winterfold, the Norse foldaen, the entrance to the underworld, and she staggers off, away through the graveyard, swearing at Ferelith and starting to cry.

'No!' she shouts. 'No way.'

Ferelith lets her go, but shouts one word after her.

'Forfeit!' she cries, triumphant. 'Forfeit!'

The Passion of Lovers

I picked the right moment, I think.

And having done that, I also picked up the gravestone and tucked it under my arm, thinking it might be a good idea to take it home.

It was only two bits of painted cardboard stuck to a thick slab of polystyrene, but I have to admit in the dark it looked pretty good.

Very realistic.

I think it did the trick.

I don't suppose I'll ever really understand everything that happened that summer. But I guess it had something to do with the way I felt about Rebecca.

I loved her.

But I hated her too.

Today is the Lord's day, and I need the Lord's love and goodness.

But like an adulterous wife who cannot look her husband in the face, I fear I have sinned beyond all redemption.

And yet, Lord, I only seek to know your design.

Is that a crime? To know the world as you have created it, as from the void, from nothing to everything; the sheep, men, trees and rivers, the mountains, women, the grass, wine, potatoes, apples, the birds of the sky, and clouds, and rain, and sun, and yes, Heaven, and angels, and . . .

And . . . ?

If you created everything, Lord, then you must have created *everything*. And everything includes demons. And devils. The Lord of Decay himself. And you must have created Hell.

Now why, Lord, would you want to do that?

Today is the Lord's day and I have never felt further from him.

And yet I must set down here what happened at the Hall last night.

He came.

The young man came, past midnight, to the Hall. He spake little, and little did the doctor speak to him, save to ask him, a threetime, whether he truly wanted to know of his future.

And each time that he was asked, all he did was to use a curse upon the Lord's name, and looking the doctor in the eye, he gave a nod.

And so this young man has become our first subject, and though my hopes were high, the results were low.

I scorn myself to record it herein, but we learned nothing.

Not a single thing.

But, oh!

The blood! The blood!

Rebecca dozes late into the morning, listening to the sound of her father downstairs, making breakfast, the radio on in the background, gently talking to no one.

She sleeps, dreams of graves, then wakes again.

Vaguely, she hears the front door closing and assumes it's her father going out, but a few moments later she hears footsteps on the stairs and for some reason, she's scared.

She sits up in bed and is about to get out when her bedroom door opens, and Ferelith walks in.

'Nice room,' she says, going straight to the window and looking at the sea.

'What the hell are you doing?' Rebecca asks, sliding out of bed and pulling her dressing gown on. 'You can't just walk into my room like that. You can't just walk into other people's houses.'

'Like you just walked into my life,' Ferelith says.

'What? What are you talking about?' Rebecca says, annoyed at having really walked straight into that one.

Ferelith shrugs.

'So, then,' she says, 'Your forfeit.'

Rebecca doesn't want to know.

'That wasn't funny,' she says. 'What you did last night. That wasn't funny.'

'Oh, come on. It was only a dare.'

'But you set me up. You must have set the whole thing up.'

Ferelith walks over to Rebecca and puts one hand out to her waist, but Rebecca pulls away.

'Stop it. I'm not happy. You scared the hell out of me.'

She sits down on the edge of the bed suddenly, and her head sinks into her hands.

Ferelith kneels by her.

'Hey,' she says. 'I'm really sorry. I didn't mean to scare you. It was just for fun, you know.'

She soothes Rebecca, whispering to her, telling her good things, saying what she needs to hear, and Rebecca starts to cry properly now.

'Hey,' says Ferelith, 'it wasn't that bad, was it?'

Rebecca shakes her head.

'It's not that. Not really. It's just . . . Everything. Everything is going wrong. I can't stand it. I can't stand it all being so hard, you know?'

Ferelith puts an arm round her. To Rebecca, still warm from her bed, Ferelith feels cold, but it's comforting nonetheless.

'I know, I do know. But you've got me. I won't let you down.'

Rebecca lays her head on Ferelith's shoulder and lets herself be held for a long time.

'Thanks,' she says, at last. 'It's good to have a friend.'

Ferelith stands up.

'Absolutely,' she says. 'And as soon as you've done your forfeit, we can be friends again.'

And with that, she leaves.

Four Sea Interludes – III

I went up to the Lover's Seat and sat by myself for a very long time.

It's a strange thing, this world of ours, I know that. But I can't work out if it makes more sense if the strangeness was created by someone (I'm talking about God here, the bad boy upstairs with the beard and the big smock thing) or whether the strangeness is just because the world is a totally random place.

And yet, the world is not totally random, is it?

Things are the way they are for a reason.

The cells of honeycombs are six-sided because a hexagon is the most material-efficient tessellation. That's just the laws of geometry and so the bees have worked that whole thing out for themselves. Which is amazing in itself, but I think Darwin had a point, you know?

I watched the waves far out to sea rolling in towards me and I thought about the pull of the moon that makes the waves in the first place, and again I thought, everything is like it is for a reason. Things are the way they are for a reason, and things happen for a reason too.

It's cause and effect.

And I think that's truest of all with people. I do something to you which makes you feel something, which makes you do something to me, or to someone else, either then, or years later.

I was thinking about that.

About how my mother went away. She was there when I went to school and when I came back all the therapy in the world had failed, and she was being carted off. So she went to that place that only made her worse and then one day (on a day when, I've always thought, she was probably feeling more sane), she managed to get herself alone for long enough to hang herself with a twisted sheet from the hot water pipes that ran along the ceiling of her room.

They boxed all the pipes up after that (because now there was a reason to do that, too).

But what I was thinking as I sat in the hot sun on the Seat, was that even that happened for a reason. She killed herself because of a long chain of reasons.

I just don't know what they were.

Rebecca spends two days sulking and feeling cross with Ferelith.

She's barely seen her father in the last week, and she wonders what he's doing with his time. More than once she smells stale beer on him.

She thinks about taking a bus into town, and walks up to the main road to the bus stop, only to find that the bus comes once a week, and not today.

She plays with her phone. Makes herself put it away, but after about five minutes gets it out again and brings up her dad's number. She doesn't call.

She puts the phone away again, and as she's walking down the shady side of the lane she's suddenly aware of the sound of someone walking behind her and turns to see Ferelith.

'What are you doing here?' she says casually.

'Same as you. Walking.'

Rebecca says nothing for a bit, then can't help herself.

'It's just a stupid game.'

'It's not.'

Rebecca stops walking.

'It is,' she says firmly.

'No, it's not,' says Ferelith, walking on. Rebecca catches her up.

'Well, what is it then?'

'It's important. It's about trust, isn't it? I trusted you. You made me do things and I did them, and I trusted you to do the same, and now you won't do your dare and you won't do the forfeit.'

'It's not like that,' Rebecca says.

'Well, that's how I see it.'

They walk in silence for a while, but the tension eases slightly and they fall into a slower step together.

'And anyway,' says Ferelith. 'You're scared.'

'Don't start that again,' Rebecca says, and then laughs.

'Sorry,' says Ferelith. 'But you know, you are full of . . .'

'Okay!' Rebecca says, laughing. 'Okay, okay, okay! I'll do it. I'll do your forfeit and then we can leave it, yes?'

Ferelith smiles.

'Good. That's good. We could go and do it now, if you want. We're close to the . . . to where we need to be.'

'Why? Where does it have to happen?'

'The Hall,' Ferelith says. 'At Winterfold Hall. It's not far from here, we could go and have a look now.'

Rebecca stops walking.

'And are you going to tell me the forfeit now?'

'When we get there. But look. It's a beautiful summer's

day. The sun in shining. "No evil can happen by daylight." Don't you know that? So you're safe. Whatever happens.'

She smiles and Rebecca tells how she'd felt as if she was in a vampire film when she first came to visit Ferelith at the Rectory. They link arms, and lean into each other, their heads touching.

Ferelith laughs, at least at first, but when Rebecca mentions the pub and the landlord, she frowns. But Rebecca doesn't notice.

'Is this going to mean more trespassing then?' she asks.

Ferelith nods.

'Good. Because I liked that.'

'You know, there's an odd thing, though. Trespassing at night feels more dangerous because it's dark, and that makes it more exciting. But it's actually more dangerous to do it in the daytime.'

'Why?'

'Because you're more likely to be seen, of course.'

'Oh yeah. So where are we trespassing then?'

'Right here.'

They've come to another point that needs repairing in the old boundary wall, and with a quick glance up and down the lane they hop over and into the overgrown wilderness of the woods.

'Are we going to the bridge again?'

'No, the Hall this time.'

They wind their way through the cool green of the trees and come into the glare on the overgrown, weed carpeted gravel that surrounds the Hall.

Rebecca inspects it, quite excited now by what she sees in front of her.

It's true, the Hall is a grand building; it rears out of the encroaching wilderness with some hint of its former majesty. The architecture is pretty wild, but not ugly, combining pale stone and red brick which somehow works together. But that's not what she notices most of all.

What she notices most of all is something she finds very hard to put into words. The Hall is old, that's obvious, but it's dead now. There's a penetrating sense that time has gone by. That everything is over. That the lives lived here have gone, never to return. Gone to the place where people go when they die. Wherever that is.

All that's left, after the people have gone, is a shell, a lifeless husk, standing like a time capsule, or maybe, more like a timeship, a place that will sail forwards through time at the rate of twenty-four hours a day, voyaging into the future, just as it has voyaged to the present day from two hundred years ago, and more.

The Hall is boarded up. Every door, every window, has thick industrial ply nailed across it, shutting the place down, sealing it like a box, blinding it as if it's sightless, stopping up its mouth so it can't tell its tales.

'It's . . .' begins Ferelith, then stops, because for once even she doesn't have the words though she's seen the Hall many times.

'Isn't it,' whispers Rebecca. 'So what happens now?'

'Follow me,' Ferelith says, leading the way.

'Are they allowed to treat an old place like this?' Rebecca asks.

'The board thing? I suppose so, or they wouldn't have done it. But it seems a shame for such an amazing old building.'

'Who owns it? Why don't they do something with it? You could turn it into a dozen luxury apartments. Be worth a fortune.'

'It's not worth a thing,' Ferelith says.

'Why not?'

They've reached the side of the house and pass a rusting and mossy old water pump, which Ferelith points out to Rebecca.

'Isn't that cool? No, it's not worth a thing. The building is unsafe, and there's no sense in spending anything on it, never mind trying to get people to pay squillions for it.'

When Rebecca still doesn't understand, Ferelith points through the woods in the direction of the cliffs.

'The sea is coming. The sea is coming. And there's absolutely nothing anyone can do about that. So this place just has to wait its turn, wait for the end. Like the rest of us.'

'But how long will that take? It could be years.'

'Maybe. Maybe more, maybe less. None of us know when our time is coming, do we? St Mary's was looking fine and then a whole chunk of cliff went. Overnight. Just like that. Three days later the east end collapsed. And that's only through the trees, over there.'

'So, what now?' Rebecca says, again, not scared, but intrigued.

Ferelith's eyes glimmer.

'Now we're going in. That's what now.'

Rebecca follows as Ferelith wanders round the Hall to the back, where she stops.

Everything is quiet and Ferelith seems to be taking time to check no one is around, walking in the woods, or on the cliff path.

'Here,' she says, and approaches one of the boarded up windows, a small one on the ground floor that's tucked away in a small courtyard. She fishes in a pocket, pulls out a penknife, and opens the blade on it, using it to pry up one corner of the boards. The nail there pops out easily and Rebecca can see it's something Ferelith has done before. She wonders when. And more importantly, why.

Ferelith puts the knife away and with both hands pulls the board from the window, just enough to squeeze through. There is no glass in the window frame. She turns to Rebecca.

'In you go.'

'But . . .'

'Quick! I can't hold this forever. And then you have to push it from inside so I can get in too.'

'But . . .'

'Quick, I said.'

And with that, and ignoring the red-stencilled lettering on the shutters saying 'DANGER: KEEP OUT!' Rebecca puts a foot on the low stone sill, and slides into Winterfold Hall.

1798, 10m, 31d.

I am a devil.

Cast me on the ground and stamp on my face with your boot, for I am a worm, a demon, a dwarf, a monster.

Yestere'en I was trialled by the Lord of Flies himself, who took me unto his bosom and made me drink of the blood, and so in this way did I come to a great bestial gluttony of both the flesh of the animal, and the flesh of woman, and having drunk my weight in wine I repaired to the house of the Widow Somers and paid her my courtesy again, and again.

Destroy me. Destroy my soul, flog it, whip it, beat it, break it and burn it and never let it see the light again, for I am an evil dog.

And in my stupor yesterday, in my orgy, I dimly perceived that the doctor came to me and whispered in my ear, close yet true.

We have another volunteer and the doctor came to tell me of this news.

The man arrives tomorrow, and so for the second time we will attempt to voyage into the other place, the unknown darkness of the afterlife.

1798, 11m, 1ð.

It is All Saints' Day, but of Saints I have seen nothing.

All I have seen is bloody horror.

He came last night, the second man.

He was older than the first, of middle years, and whereas our first visitor was taciturn, this newcomer spoke freely.

He came early in the dead morning to us.

He was greatly vexed and displayed a deal and a measure of agitation.

The doctor made efforts to calm him, and offered him wine and something more in the wine perhaps, but though he tried, the man would not listen to the doctor's ministrations.

He wanted mine. He wanted the man of God to offer solace and explanation.

He turned to me and he was shaking.

– Will I see an angel, Father? said he. Will I see an angel to take me to heaven?

I oped my mouth but I spake not.

The doctor stood behind him, and nodded at me, with great ferocity, urging me to answer.

So I answered him.

- Have you been a God-fearing man? I asked, and he told me that he had.

- Then, I said. You will see an angel, and he will take you to Heaven when the time comes. When the time comes.

And with that the man was calmed, and we led him like a docile creature of the field, a lamb, into the Candle Room.

We bound him to the chair, now with shackles at wrist and ankle. We placed the candles on the floor, and we locked the door behind him, and we walked along the corridor to the unseen room.

Again, there came that awful elapse of time in which we waited, and waited, and though I saw not its purpose, the doctor explained to me carefully again its necessity in ensuring the physiology of our subject was at an optimum.

I understood not.

- The realm of the soul is yours, he said. But the realm of the body is mine. So leave that to my care.

Pattern recognition

None of it was that hard. Not when you have the resources I have, by which I mean to say, when you're as smart as I am.

You can have *anything*, but you won't be as strong as me if you're not as smart as me. That's the way I see it. All those dumb kids at school, all the dumb teachers. All the dumb people I've had to put up with at the Rectory. They could be stronger than me, or have more money than me, or be better looking than me, but they don't win in the end, because I have one thing above all else that makes me better.

My mind.

I see everything. I see the patterns in life that make us who we are. One day I will know everything, and when I do, I will be utterly powerful. Because when you know everything about people, and why they are the way they are, you know the way they will react in any given situation, and you know how to lead them, this way or that, to do the things you want them to do.

And that's more powerful than looks, or money, or physical strength.

I know that, but Rebecca didn't.

Rebecca waits as Ferelith climbs in after her, then can't hold back the plywood boards any more, and they snap back, shutting them in, shutting out the light.

'Don't you have that torch?' Rebecca asks, her voice edgy.

'Nope,' Ferelith says. 'Didn't think we'd be coming here today.'

Not for the first time, Rebecca wonders whether Ferelith is telling her the truth.

'But how are we going to see? Perhaps this isn't a good idea. Let's come back later when . . .'

'No!' Ferelith insists. 'You're not going to back out again.'

'I'm not backing out, I just think it's crazy when we can't see. I promise I'll do whatever it is you want. Later. When we have a torch.'

'Do you have your mobile?'

'Yes, but . . .'

'Good. We can use the light from the screen.'

Rebecca is beaten and she knows it. She rummages in her pocket and pulls her mobile out, hitting a button on the keypad as she does, lighting up the little screen, and the small space they're standing in.

It's some kind of pantry, or storeroom. The window they climbed through never had glass in it but a wooden louvre, now long rotted and mostly gone.

It's cold. There's thick dust under their feet, and some pungent smell, but with an acrid edge, like vinegar.

The light from the phone goes out.

'Push it again,' Ferelith says, but Rebecca already has.

'I don't have much battery,' she says.

'That's okay,' Ferelith says. 'We won't need it for long. And anyway, you're not planning on making any calls, are you?'

It goes out, and as Rebecca turns it on again, Ferelith snatches it.

'Hey!'

'I'm just going to change the settings. You can change how long the backlight stays on for, can't you?'

She stabs a few buttons and seems satisfied.

'There we are.'

'Can I have it back?' Rebecca asks.

'Better if I have it for now,' Ferelith says. 'I'm going to lead the way and it's pretty dangerous in here. You have to watch for the floorboards. Some of them aren't there any more.'

'You've been here before?' Rebecca asks, even though she knows the answer.

'Yes. Of course I have. Watch your step and put your feet where mine go.'

'Where are we going?'

'Inside.'

'We are inside.'

'Really inside.'

Ferelith nudges the door to the little room open with her foot and heads out.

They're in kitchens, Rebecca can see that, even though there are no modern appliances, no cookers or fridges. She sees a large sink almost the size of a bath, long wooden work surfaces, sharp meat hooks hanging from rails along the walls.

Rebecca wonders when a meal was last cooked in these kitchens. How many people came to dinner. What they ate, and whether they liked it, and whether it was a happy evening.

It's so dead here, the sense of loss, of decay, of long years of nothingness, that Rebecca thinks she might scream, but fortunately Ferelith doesn't stop to sightsee, and crosses the floor by the most direct route to a door on the far side.

They leave the kitchens behind.

Ferelith seems to know where she's going, but she's not in a rush to get to wherever that might be.

'So,' Rebecca says, but her voice dries up and she has to start again. 'So, where are we going? Is it far?'

She tries to inject a lightness that she doesn't feel into her voice.

'Not far,' says Ferelith. 'There's some cool stuff to see too, but mostly the place was emptied when it was shut down.'

'When was that?'

'The fifties, I think.'

'The nineteen fifties?'

'Yeah, why?'

'Because it feels like no one's been here in centuries. Why did they shut it up?'

'Someone died.'

'Shut up. Don't try to scare me.'

'No. I just mean someone who owned it died and there was no one who wanted to take it on. It might look like it's worth a fortune, but like I said, it's not worth a thing because when the sea comes, that's it.'

Ferelith slips down a corridor, holding Rebecca's phone in front of her, casting an eerie glow on the desolation that waits for them.

'It would cost you more to repair the place than you'd ever get back from it. That's all I meant. Though having said that,' she says, 'there have always been stories about this place. Aside from the one about the doctor. It's been empty on and off. Before the last owner died, it was used as a hospital for wounded American airmen. In the Second World War. There were loads of airbases around here, and they took over places like this to be hospitals. They turned all the big rooms into wards.'

'That's weird. Didn't the owners mind?'

'They didn't have any choice. And anyway, everyone had to suffer in the war, didn't they? Even the rich.'

She turns a corner and Rebecca hurries after the firefly light.

Coming around the corner she can see they're in a bigger space but the light of the phone isn't strong enough to show her how big.

There are other clues though. The air sounds wider around them, not as claustrophobic, and it's cooler again too. Rebecca's eyes search the space and she realises that her phone isn't the only light.

'Let it go out,' she says, and Ferelith hides the phone in her pocket.

There actually is some other light.

They're in the entrance hall, and sunbeams in which the dust dances like tiny moths spear through tiny chinks in the boards. There's a different smell here, different from the kitchens and the pantry. This smell is really unpleasant, as if there are rats decaying under the floorboards. And worse.

'Isn't that pretty?' Ferelith says, watching the narrow rods of sunlight stabbing down, the bright hot sun outside reduced to this backdrop of stars.

'That's how our sun would look from another galaxy,'

she adds. 'Nothing more than one tiny star among millions. A pin prick.'

Rebecca shudders. It's cold in the Hall, and she's only wearing a vest top, because it's been another beast of a sunny day. Only now does she wonder why Ferelith is wearing a hoodie. She must have been baking outside.

'Can we get on with this?' Rebecca asks, still wondering what it is that she will have to do. She thinks about her father for some reason that she can't place. She doesn't feel angry with him, she doesn't feel sad. What she feels is nothing.

'Yeah,' says Ferelith. 'Sorry. This way, I think.'

She turns and flicks the phone back on, heading into the bowels of the building and away from the weak light.

They walk down a long corridor and make a couple of turns. Now the silence is complete but for their breathing and the creak of the boards under their feet, and the darkness is total but for the light from the phone.

'Come on,' Ferelith says. 'This way. We're nearly there.'

'Where?'

'The Candle Room.'

Candle

We came down the hallway and though I knew my way in the dark by then, I made a bit of a show of having to stop and think, and remembering the right way, and so on.

I think I managed to make it look like an accident that we came to the Candle Room. I pulled aside the boards that I'd replaced after my previous visit, remembering the day I made, in my opinion, the greatest archaeological discovery since they found that Viking boat burial down the road in the thirties.

I found the door handle and gave it a sharp tug. It's stiff and needs a bit of force, but then I barged the door open and we were inside.

I sniffed the air, and as usual, it stank of decay. Truth is, the inside of the Hall is such a riot of different horrible smells that one more terrible smell was neither here nor there.

'Is this it?'

I told her it was.

'So what do I have to do then?' she asked.

I was about to tell her, when the phone's light went out.

'God!' I said.

185

'What?' she asked, and I could hear the panic in her voice.

'Phone's dead. Damn. Listen, don't worry. It's only darkness. We can get out of here. It'll be easy if we're careful.'

'No,' she said. 'No. I don't like this. I want the light back on. Give me my phone.'

'I told you,' I said. 'It's dead. No point.'

'I don't care. I want my phone back. Give it to me.'

I heard her move and thought I should tell her to be careful.

'There's things on the floor in here,' I explained. 'You ought to watch your step.'

She stopped, and swore.

'Look,' I said. 'Let me sort it. Stay where you are, I'll come and find you. And don't panic.'

'Hurry,' she said, and I knew she was spooked.

I stretched my fingers out ahead of me, stroking the air till I touched her.

'There. Look, there's something behind you.'

I felt around in the dark with my foot and found the chair.

'Sit down here,' I said.

I was calm, but firm, just how you should talk to people who are panicking.

'Why?' she asked.

'Because then you'll be safe and won't hurt yourself on anything while I find some light.'

186

I gave her a gentle push, just to encourage her, and sure enough, she sat down.

Then it only took a moment to do it.

I found her wrists and flicked the bracelets over them before she even knew what I was doing.

'Hey!' she cried. 'Ferelith!'

She yelled at me then, because she immediately knew something was wrong, but I was already fixing the hoops round her ankles, and as she felt them tighten, she really started to lose it.

'Hey!' I shouted. 'Hey! Rebecca! Hey!'

'What the hell are you doing?' she yelled in the darkness.

But then it wasn't dark any more, because I pulled her phone back out of my pocket, and flicked the light on once more.

'You said that was dead!' she said, as if the fact that I'd lied was the worst thing I could have done.

And maybe it was.

Then.

'What are you doing?' she screamed. 'Let me go.'

'No,' I said. 'It's time for your forfeit. It's time to find out if you've been a good girl, or a bad girl. I wonder who's coming for you. The Angel or the Devil?'

1798, 12m, 3d.

Behold!

Death and eternity, and a doom just and uncaring are at the door. Lord, be merciful.

A sweet calm lies upon the land, the white snows have come to lay a virginal sheet upon everything, so that even the cattle shed and the byre are things of beauty.

But this beauty brings no relief from suffering, for the village freezes, and the poor struggle to warm themselves at feeble fires made of thin kindling.

This cold has held the land fast in its grip these past weeks, and yet I feel it not.

I feel no cold. I feel heat. I feel the heat of the pit. I feel the heat of Satan's breath upon the back of my neck. I feel his eyes scorch my soul.

Further, I feel the warmth of human blood as I, as we, toil in Winterfold Hall, I bathe in rivers of hot human blood as we continue to explore.

My Holy Christ!

I had no idea, I freely confess, of the physical nature of man.

I see now I had merely a superficial knowledge of the workings of the human machine. I did not know about these various things that the doctor has shown me.

I did not know about veins, and their cousins, the arteries. I did not know about muscles, and tendons and ligaments. I did not know of the spinal cord upon which the head sits. Such a strong thing is the neck, and yet, ultimately, not so very hard to break. Not so very hard at all.

And I did not know about the blood.

I knew of course, that there is blood to be found in a human, but I had little idea of its utter quantity.

There is so much of it. So very much of the hot, thick stuff.

And so I understood why the doctor had gone to the trouble of introducing the series of grates and sluices in the lower chamber.

But, O Lord. My spirits are weak.
It has been five now.
Five.

1798, 12m, 5d.

What yet do we lack?
Why are the secrets denied to us?
What more can we do?

I left the house this afternoon. I found Martha skulking in the kitchens, and though I bid her cheerily tell me what lay in store for my supper, she merely grunted a reply. She has been this way several times of late and I wonder what has occurred in her.

So I left the house, and I turned to the church, and sought refuge there. I sat, as before, in the pews of the common man, and I lifted my eyes to the holy of holies, but my soul looked down, through the flags at my feet, down to the evil hidden, way below.

I stirred, and dragged myself from the pews to my pulpit. I climbed the narrow wooden stair, unhooked the gate and stood my ground, as I must have done on many thousands of days.

I rested my hands on the edge of the pulpit and tried to summon something within me. I occasioned to think of the many times when I had found the Holy Spirit enter me in my pulpit, and yet these moments seemed as fleeting and as meaningless as the dreams of a dead man.

I was alone.

I had tried to summon the Lord, and yet He deserted me.

I thought of other summonings, less noble ones, devilish and ill-starred, and I thought of the five who had come and gone, now.

Each had expected a summoning. Each praying for an angel, yet fearing the Devil would come, and each the biggest fool in Christendom.

Fools, all five.

Each one the doctor had asked.

Three times, that they should be sure they knew what they faced.

And yet each was fooled.

For none of them knew what it was that truly came upon them.

Not one suspected the truth, the truth that it was neither an angel nor a devil who would come to greet them, but a piece of burnished French steel, a foot across; as sharp as Lucifer's mind and as hard as his heart.

At two in the morning, rose and worshipped, but did not worship the Lord. Instead I went to the Hall and bowed down before what the doctor will have me call Science.

So I worshipped Science, and I saw what Science would deliver unto me, but as yet this new god had been as parsimonious as the Lord has been to me hitherto.

This god Science had shown us nothing of the other side, all he has shown us is the hideous spectacle that is the inner workings of the human engine.

And yet.

Last night, as we worshipped at the altar of Science, something happened that has given us renewed vigour.

And an answer must come at last, because we cannot I fear continue with our work for very much longer before rumours seek us out and destroy us.

Last night was number six.

But at long last we have a start!

I confess that I had begun to doubt the doctor's skills, despite all he had instructed me on the lore he had discovered in his years of training in Paris.

I doubt him no longer.

We stood before the chair, such a brute of a construction, sitting on the rails that carry deep into the lower chamber, where all sound may go unheard.

The chair, aside from the shackles at wrist and elbow, is a simple enough throne, of solid oak, but it holds no great secret, nor mystery.

But when it departs the Candle Room, and takes its run underground, coming to rest against the other half of its being, then it truly becomes a machine for crossing the barriers to the afterlife.

It is here that the doctor's greatest skills of physiology and the mechanic arts combine. It is here the blade that the doctor witnessed at first hand in the Terror in Paris is put to use, as the chair runs to meet the stop, whereon the blade is fixed.

Waiting.

And as I sluiced the blood away once more, I marvelled at what we had seen.

As before, the victim came willingly. It is true to say that the man was afeared, but merely for his future soul, not his present life.

Three times the doctor bade him.

– Are you willing?

And three times the man answered that he was.

As with so many of the others, he turned to me and

wanted the Lord's blessing on the proceedings.

We bid him go to the chair, and he settled in to meet his fate.

The candles lit, we retired, and set to waiting.

The doctor had been experimenting with the time involved, and had shortened the candle stubs, so it was not more than one hour till the final flame flickered in the dark and died.

From the hidden room behind the panel, I called to him.

– And are you a God-fearing man?

And then we threw the lever, and throwing ourselves upon the wheeled dollies we had made, hurtled through the darkness after his retreating body.

By the time we arrived, it was done.

The blade had done its work, and once again, neatly bisected the head from the body, and yet, by the doctor's great art, left it resting on the blade, so that very little difference could be discerned at first, save the release of some blood from the pressure within.

This, the doctor has told me oft, is the secret to his system, so that while the man was truly dead (for who can live with a blade between his body and his head?), there was still the opportunity afforded us to communicate.

The man was dead, and yet now the doctor leaned in close by the lamplight, and called to him.

'Underhill! Underhill! Do you hear me? Do you hear me?'

And now, finally, did we perceive success.

For his eyes opened. Wide.

They shut again, and the doctor called again, urgently.

'Underhill! Hear me! What do you see? What do you see?'

The eyelids of the dead man did open once more, and the eyes swivelled to look the doctor in the face, but inches away.

His eyes fixed the doctor, but this was not an end to the miracles before us, for then, O Lord, his lips twitched, and parted, so slightly.

And we thought that he was to speak to us, but no utterance came, and the mouth closed again, and then the eyes became as dull as stone, and our moment was gone.

Such success! Such glory!

And yet the final glory still denied to us, for whatever it was that Underhill had seen he had failed to tell us.

I thought long on this tonight.

I saw Underhill's staring eyes, as he tried to speak to us from beyond the grave.

What did he see?

Clouds and angeldust?

Or devils and hellfires?

What did he see?

All I know is what I saw of him, the look on his face, which it has taken me all evening to put a name to.

The name I have now, and it is this: surprise.

R ebecca has given up shouting now.
All that's left is fear and confusion. Her heart is
thumping as though she's a frightened rabbit in a cage,
and maybe that's just what she is.

Before Ferelith left her, she'd wandered round the
chair, and from a darkened corner of the room had
produced a five-branched candelabra.

She'd placed it in front of Rebecca's feet, but out of
reach. Then she'd gone to a high narrow rail that ran
round the whole room, and rummaging, her fingers
closed on something she had obviously put there earlier.

She'd rattled the matchbox as she'd come back over to
Rebecca, and bending down, had calmly lit the five candles.

And then she'd gone, and all Rebecca's pleading and
shouting and threatening and begging had done no good
at all.

All Ferelith had said was, 'Farewell, sweet love.'

Now Rebecca waits, and watches the flames of the
candles.

She wonders how long the candles will last, and

whether Ferelith will come back before they go out.

She's sitting in a windowless room, in the centre of a derelict manor house, and she's shackled to a chair that's bolted to the floor. She knows this because she has tried to stand and lift the chair, but it wouldn't move any more than she can. She's been tied to the chair by someone she thought was her friend, but now she has no idea who, or what, Ferelith is. No one else knows she's in the Hall, and even if she could get free, she doesn't have her phone. The only light in the room is coming from five flickering candles set in a candelabra on the floor in front of her, and just as she's thinking these things, the first of them, which was very short, splutters and goes out.

Suddenly, with no other explanation, she knows what's going on. Ferelith intends her to stay in the room until all five candles have gone out. She wants her to wait for an angel or a devil.

Rebecca laughs, but it's not a laugh with any joy in it.

She sees that this is another of Ferelith's freaky games, and she's fallen for it. She knows there are no such things as angels, and certainly knows that there are no such things as devils. She's not some ignorant country bumpkin from the past who might have believed in such things, she knows there's nothing to be scared of. She tells herself this three times, just to be sure.

Nothing to be scared of.

Nothing.

Be scared.

Ferelith had told her the legend of the Hall, of this room.

If the legend were true, then somewhere is a place where Ferelith is sitting watching her, just as the doctor waited for his victim's end, and she suddenly looks round the room again, staring through the gloom at the walls.

She can see nothing, but the thought that Ferelith might be watching her through some slit or grille makes her mad again.

'Ferelith!' she yells, startled by the strength of her own voice, startled by the fear in it. 'Ferelith! If you're there . . . You listen to me. You come and let me out right now! Let me out now and I'll forget about it. Ferelith! Ferelith? Are you there? If you're watching me, I swear . . .'

She stops, and then suddenly the panic rises in her throat, bubbling up from her beating heart, throwing itself out of her mouth with rage and anger, and she screams.

She screams, a desperate, incoherent scream. A shriek, and then she screams something that terrifies her. It terrifies her because she means it.

'Ferelith! I'll kill you!'

She screams again and then her head hangs and she begins sobbing, and before long she's choking on her tears and snot, unable to wipe it away, since she's bound to a chair in a darkened room.

199

Four Sea Interludes – IV

I went for a walk, because to tell the truth I find it a bit creepy in the Hall. It's dark and dusty and there's this whole feel about it. Like an aura, but not an aura of light, an aura of sucking darkness.

I went to the Lover's Seat and sat in the sun and fiddled with Rebecca's phone. After a while I got too hot and took my hoodie off and it was nice to feel the sun on my shoulders and arms.

I scrolled through her address book but nothing was very interesting.

Then I went to her inbox and looked through her texts. The most recent ones were from me, and I noted that she'd deleted some of mine, but not others. She'd kept ones where I'd said something nice, like one where I called her *Best of Friends*. I scrolled down to a couple from her dad, and again she'd kept boring ones which said *I love you*, or *You are my angel*, that kind of thing. It kind of makes me sick, apart from the fact that I liked the way he called her an angel.

Because if Rebecca was an angel, then that must make me the devil. That made me laugh.

Then I found some texts from Adam, the boy. She was

holding on to them, though why she'd want to do that when he'd dumped her I don't know.

They were the usual mushy stuff.

Miss you! xxx

Hey. I was just about to text you! I love you too x

I'm always happy to hear from you. Call me? X

The usual mush.

Then I checked her sent items, because lots of people forget to delete the texts they've sent, and to my great joy I discovered that Rebecca was one of them.

The battery gave me a warning beep then, and I knew I wouldn't have long.

There they all were.

Texts to me. Texts to her dad.

I hate you. How can you be my father?

What am I supposed to do? I don't know what to say.

And an older one.

Daddy. Please tell me that what they're saying isn't true. Please.

That had to be about the start of the case, when it hit the papers. I checked the date on the text and it pretty much fitted with what I remembered reading. So Rebecca must have been at school with all her friends when the news came out about how her dad made the wrong decision, and how he called off the team that were investigating the woods, and how if he hadn't they might have found that girl tied to a table in a hut. While she was still alive, that is.

Then I found some texts to Adam, and among them I suddenly realised she was talking about me.

It's okay for you. I'm stuck here with a freak. She's weird.

I looked out to sea.

I watched the blue-grey waves heaving and felt like going for a swim, but I knew there wasn't really time for that. I had to get back to the Hall.

Eventually.

Maybe.

I played with my knife for a bit, stabbing the dry earth around me, digging up the dusty soil, idly thinking about sun and rain. Lots of the first, none of the second. And me being a freak.

I stabbed the dry ground again, and I thought about Rebecca and Adam. Texting about me.

I was just doing that when her phone rang.

It surprised me so much that I dropped it. I picked it up again and read the display.

Dad.

I answered it.

'Hello?' he said.

'Hello, Mr Case,' I said. 'Your daughter is with the angels now. Or the devils.'

And that's when the phone died, the battery finally gone.

1798, 12m, 10d.

A Christless day today.

We toiled hard and long, but I was merely an innocent. I had become a simple labourer in the employ of Dr Barrieux.

The doctor was in a foul and sunken mood, and he spoke little, indeed, he spoke only to give me further command or direction.

And Lord! The reek and stench from the lower chamber is becoming unbearable. Our coffins are thin and makeshift, and do not keep as much in as we had hoped. The air in the chamber has become noxious, and though we wore wettened kerchiefs across nose and mouth, it was poor defence against the onslaught of putrefaction.

The day ended. The doctor straightened his back as we pulled ourselves from the tunnel and back into the candle room.

– So, he said, and he looked at me with a level countenance. Tonight will make number seven, will it not?

– It shall, I agreed.

– Then let us pray that seven is a holy number, a number of God, and that we achieve success tonight?

– Pray? I enquired. Pray? God? Since when have these been your methods?

And at this the doctor had no answer, but hung his head, and disappeared into the Hall proper.

We had several hours to dispense with before our seventh investment arrived, but I did not fancy to return to the Rectory, so I made a turn about the various rooms of the Hall, and read awhile in the library. There I found a translation of a long poem from the Italian tongue, by a man named Dante.

And therein the most accurate and terrifying depictions of Hell I have ever read. I was dumbfounded, struck with mortal terror, and my soul was torn with dismay.

It seems that Hell is far more complex in its multifarious horrors than I ever have imagined. I read of the various circles and planes of the damned, and the appalling and unbelievable tortures that await us there.

I read for hours, then could read no more. I slammed the book shut and lay it back on its shelf with a trembling hand, but though I had closed the covers of the book, what I had read remained burned across my brain like the branding fork of the Devil on the buttocks of the sinner.

I had spent too much time, brooding on my own self. For as I wandered around the Hall, I thought that I heard some other presence in the rooms, thought I saw something stir behind a curtain, and knew that I was imagining things. More than once I thought I caught the shape of a small figure, a boy, from the corner of my eye.

I found the doctor later, and he was drunk, half-asleep on the couch, and in his arms he cradled the portraits of his wife and his daughter.

His cheeks were caked with dried tears.

I prodded his shoulder roughly.

– Doctor.

He stirred not.

– Doctor! Awake!

This time he stirred.

– The time is nearly here. Come. We have work to do.

And so he rose to do that work.

Rebecca's body aches, cramps have come and gone in both legs and arms, but her neck is the worst. It aches so badly, and she thinks again about how long it's been. She has no idea.

Though she's wearing a watch, she can't see the face. She decides to count for a while, doing maths in her head. If she can count to sixty fairly accurately, that's a minute. So if she can count to three hundred, that's five minutes.

While she counts, she stares at the candles.

She's got to six hundred before she starts crying again. None of the candles seem to have burned any way down at all.

Unwelcome notions wander into her head.

Will Ferelith come back before the candles have gone out? Is she coming back at all?

It's the first time she's permitted that thought to exist, and though she tries to push it away, like all bad thoughts, it won't be banished easily. It keeps rising in her mind, and every time it does, it gets stronger.

Supposing Ferelith has left her here?

For good.

She tries not to think it, but fails, so then she decides to let herself think about it, but rationally.

People don't do that kind of thing, she tells herself, people don't do bad things like that. Not in the real world, but as soon as she thinks that, she thinks about the girl tied to the table in the hut in the woods. Rebecca knows her father stopped looking for that girl. Supposing he were to stop looking for her too?

She lifts her head and stares at the candles, the four remaining candles, and at last she sees that they have burned lower.

One of them is quite short now, and as Rebecca stares at it, she convinces herself that she can see it actually burning down.

She's close enough to the candelabra to see the life of the flame.

The candle is creamy yellow-white. The wick is whiter where it's not burned, and black where the flame has it. The flame is . . . The flame is amazing, and she becomes entranced by it as she realises she's never looked at a flame properly.

What colour is it?

It's yellow, she thinks, then realises that there is no name for the yellow-orange-white-gold-blue that a candle flame burns. Its shape is perfect, and it flutters in an unfelt breeze, a draft so gentle that only something as delicate as the candle flame can be moved by it.

And yet the flame is strong. It has burned for hours. It sucks up the molten wax from the bowl formed in the top of the candle stub, and steadily eats it all away, drop by drop.

There's barely any wax left now in this candle, and Rebecca expects it go out some time soon, but it doesn't. Despite everything that's happening to her, she still has the energy to be amazed as the candle enters an extremely long series of death throes, as the last of the solid wax slips onto the stem of the candlestick, and yet the wick remains feeding a flame that now gets bigger if anything, feeding it till it sputters and gutters around the silver lip of the candlestick.

A thousand times it appears as if it will die, and doesn't, and then from nowhere, it's gone.

There are three candles left.

She watches them briefly, then she's distracted as she realises she needs to pee, and knows there's no chance of that happening in any way she would like.

She's cold too. As the heat of the day outside seems impossibly far away now. She shivers, and a new fear surges through her, a fear that is totally ridiculous, but which she cannot destroy.

She thinks about the legend of the Candle Room. Despite everything she thinks she knows, despite the fact that this is the twenty-first century, maybe she's wrong. Most people in the world still believe in God. They don't believe in the same one, not all of them, though Christians and Catholics and Jews do. And she remembers from World Studies that Allah isn't so very different from the Christian God. But then there are Buddhists and Taoists, and Hindus and Sikhs. And she supposes, there are Pagans and Wiccans and that kind of thing. And most of the world believes in some kind of god, and if they're right, and she's wrong, what then?

If there is heat, there must be cold.

If there is light, there must be dark.

And if there is God, and a phalanx of angels, then there must also be the Devil.

And as she watches the third candle go out, and the room becomes even dimmer and darker, she suddenly thinks that if she's wrong, and six billion other people in the world are right, then maybe something is going to come and get her when that last candle goes out.

As she sits in the chair and she tries for the twentieth time to pull her wrists out of the shackles, tugging and straining and failing and swearing, she's overtaken by the horribly real sensation that there is something in the room with her, behind her, unseen.

The fourth candle goes quite quickly.

'Who's there?' she calls out. 'Who's there? Who is it?'

Nothing.

Except, does she hear a noise somewhere outside the room? It's gone, whatever it was; mouse or rat. Or Ferelith.

'Ferelith? Is that you?'

She's so tired now, she can't even be angry, she can't even shout.

She sits still and quiet, and the feeling that someone is there with her slides gently away. But what if there had been someone? What if someone had entered the room? And what about when the last candle goes?

She looks at it, as if it's her enemy, but maybe it's her friend.

She has nothing else now. No one else.

Everyone has gone.

Her father, who let her down.

Her friends, who were only there when it suited them.

Adam, who never really cared.

Ferelith, who has actually left her to die in darkness. She remembers the conversation they had a couple of weeks ago. At the time, she took it for another weird conversation with Ferelith, but now it takes on more significance. Ferelith had told her about the man who wrote the Sherlock Holmes stories. She knows them, but she doesn't remember the author's name. Ferelith told her how this writer made a pact with his brother, the ultimate experiment, so that when one of them died, he would find a way to contact the other, to tell him that the afterlife was real.

'We could do that, too,' Ferelith said. 'Wouldn't that be cool?'

And Rebecca had smiled and agreed because well, Ferelith wanted to, and, what harm could it do?

'Do you mean it?' Ferelith said. And only now does Rebecca realise that she meant it.

She's tired, she's cold, she's hungry, with nothing left in her life but the single spluttering candle flame. Her thoughts grow wild.

The Devil deals with darkness. His tools, she thinks, are the things of shadow. He can only live in the dark places, and he uses the play of illusion to create his monsters, which can only be destroyed by the light of God.

Has she been a good girl, she wonders? Has she led a good life?

Who is coming for her when her candle dies?

She knows she's done some bad things, but nothing terrible. She's let a few people down, and she's told a few lies, but mostly to avoid other people's feelings being hurt. She stole a mobile phone case from the market once. She felt so bad about it the following day she threw it away.

And she's done some good things.

She's sure she has. It's just that she can't think of any of them right now, that's all.

And while she's thinking all that, she starts to see shapes in the candle flame, sooty shadows of devils dancing in the smoke that twists up away from the tip of the flame.

She sees angels and she sees them speared by devils with tridents in their hands, and grins on their lips. She sees them dance and leap and laugh and stab their spears. An angel tries to wave a sword of light at them, but they surround him, sneering and laughing as they pin him down, and set light to his hair, and put a burning flame to his flesh too.

The angel dies.

The flame of the candle performs a last mad dance, and then, in a puff of smoke that goes unseen in the dark, it dies too.

The room is dark.

And a voice calls through the darkness to Rebecca.

1798, 12m, 11d.

I returned from last night's labours with a heavy heart.

Our seventh investment was a man from Winterfold itself, by the name of Mason.

He was old, soon to be taken, and desperate to know what lay in store for him. He questioned me continually, but would not look the doctor in the eye.

– If it's the worst, Father, is it too late? Can I do aught to change my lot? I shall repent. I shall repent! I shall do everything that I might do to change my lot, Father. I'm a good man. I'm a good man.

Thus did he prattle, without end, and I bid him be still, and told him that there is always the chance for the evil man to repent, and to do good, so that he may come to God and be spared at the day of judgement.

This silenced him a little, but the French steel silenced him even more, for, God! He screamed as the chair ran back down its rails to the lower chamber. He screamed as though the very Devil himself was upon his breast, chewing at his throat.

But he became silent enough when the blade cut into his neck.

We were hard upon him at the very moment of his passing, and yet the scream did not merely die, but was cut short, a most eerie effect.

We studied his visage, and again the doctor called to him.

– Mason! Mason! Speak to us! What do you see?

His eyelids opened, and the orbs swivelled to stare not at the doctor, but at me.

He fixed me with a stare that lasted for a full half-minute, during which time his lips twitched and moved as if to speak, but no sound came.

And I bethought me of the deaf man, who has learned to read words from the movements of another's lips, though he does not himself hear a single utterance.

And though I tried and I struggled to see the shape of his words, I could not. It was a tantalising thing, for in the play of his lips, were words I knew, and yet I could not bring them to mind.

And then his eyes closed, and he was gone from us forever.

– Prepare the coffin, spake the doctor and I moved away around the tiny lower chamber to make ready with the rough box, gagging on the smell as I did.

Our work done, I returned home, and slept late, and though the morning was frosty, the reception I had from Martha was frostier still.

Finally my patience was worn through.

– Heavens! I pronounced with full vigour and ire. What is come over you?

But she spake not, and so, Lord, I struck her on the cheek.

– Answer me!

And she shouted back at me then.

– You are at the Devil's work, are you not? Are you not?

Waiting for the Spirits

I figured she'd had enough by then. So when the last flame went out, I called through the grille in the wall of the Candle Room.

'And are you a God-fearing girl?'

She screamed, which was kind of funny and kind of scary, and then there was silence. I guess that was her realising it was me, recognising my voice, and then she started yelling and shouting and swearing at me.

I came in through the door and put the lamp I'd brought from home down on the floor.

She blinked and screwed her eyes up but she didn't stop shouting at me.

'Jeez,' I said, 'calm down. It was just your forfeit. That's all.'

But she really wouldn't calm down, and I had to get her to shut up so I told her I would only let her out if she stopped shouting and swearing and everything.

'Look,' I said, 'it was just a laugh, just your forfeit. I said you had to do a forfeit, didn't I? You didn't take it seriously, did you? Did you?'

I laughed then, which probably wasn't a good idea,

because she got really cross again. She called me all sorts of things. She called me a freak, which hurt. But then, I already knew that's what she thought of me.

I stopped laughing and I told her I wasn't going to let her out. Ever.

Then she started crying, so I did let her out and I started crying too, and we put our arms round each other and I said I was really, really sorry, and that it was only supposed to be a game, but I was sorry if I'd hurt her and so on.

And I wanted her to be sorry she'd hurt me, but I didn't say anything about that. Not yet.

She calmed down a bit, and then she suddenly began hitting me and screaming at me again. I shoved her back and we wrestled in a clumsy way. Then I was strong enough to hold her off and after a while she stopped fighting and started sobbing again.

I held her some more and it was really nice to be so close to her, and smell her smell.

And the best thing? The best thing was that I could feel she needed me. Totally.

She stood up, and looked around the room, as if she'd never seen it before, which I guess she hadn't, not properly.

It was quite boring, to tell the truth.

Yeah, it has some cute wood panelling and all, but there's nothing else to see, except the heavy chair, stuck to the floor.

'Look,' I said, 'isn't it weird?'

'What?' she asked, but she was miles away, her voice was all thin and dull.

'The chair. It's bolted to the floor. You know I found this place? The Hall had been boarded up in the fifties, but the door to this room was behind some panelling that looked much older. Someone hid this place. It's underneath the main stairway, so you wouldn't really see that a room was missing. But look at the floor, see where the chair is fixed. The floor looks funny there, like there's something underneath, but I've never been able to find out what.'

I stopped. She clearly couldn't care less.

'Don't you want to know? If you helped me, maybe we could find out.'

Then she said the worst thing she could have done, and I knew that my feeling of a few moments before had been a lie. She didn't want me at all. She didn't need me.

She hated me.

'Ferelith,' she said. 'I only want you to show me the way out of this place, and then I never want to see you again, as long as I live. Right?'

It takes two days before Rebecca realises that her father's heart is missing.

She knows she was wearing the pendant when she went in, she knows she was wearing it as she sat bound to the chair, but now it's gone.

For reasons she only dimly understands, she's shocked by the loss. It takes her quite a while longer to think calmly about where it might have got lost, and when she does, she knows immediately.

She remembers the fight with Ferelith. That mad struggle after she'd been set free, and as she replays it in her head, she knows that her subconscious mind registered something that she did not. She feels a sudden tug at her neck, and knows that her father's heart got pulled off in the fight, and is lying on the floor of the Candle Room, in the dark.

Two weeks have passed since she ran from the Hall. It's a slow and hateful time, which drags its sorry carcass through the days. Every waking second is torture to Rebecca. She had no idea that time could pass with such slowness and such pain, and yet each new morning dawns with a terrible vista to be got through, somehow or other.

Her father does no more than exist in the same house.

The evening she returned from the Candle Room, she ran straight into his arms, and cried, but when he asked what was wrong, she didn't answer.

'It's that girl, isn't it?' he'd said, but Rebecca had said nothing.

Her father had persisted.

'She answered your phone, didn't she? I knew it was her. What was she doing with your phone?'

Still Rebecca had said nothing, just backed away from him, closing in on herself.

'What have you been doing? Has she upset you?'

'Just leave me alone,' Rebecca said, heading upstairs.

'That's right,' her father had shouted, 'that's right. I

don't have any other choice, though, do I? What else can I do? You won't bloody talk to me, will you?'

'What do you want me to say? You're not here. You're not actually here, are you? Don't you know how . . .'

'What? Don't I know what? If you ever talked to me and not that freakish girl maybe I would know. I tell you right now, Rebecca, I want you to stop seeing her. You understand me? You stop seeing her right now. I can't be dealing with any more rubbish. Haven't you got a moment to wonder what I'm going through?'

And with that Rebecca stormed upstairs, yelling as she went.

'And don't you know how lonely I am!'

She'd gone, leaving her father staring angrily at the evening light through the kitchen window.

Since then, all pretence of being a family has been abandoned.

So it passes, two weeks of Rebecca's life stretching into an eternity. She withdraws into herself, and though she doesn't realise it's happening, her mind changes. It darkens, it shrinks, it closes down, it becomes a wounded animal looking for a place to hide.

Her thoughts become by turns frantic and desperate, then abnormally quiet and still. She feels as if she's a zombie, but she knows she hurts too much to really be dead.

And then it happens.

Her father doesn't come home one night.

She waits, uninterested at first, but as the hours crawl by, she starts to grow afraid.

When her phone rings, she leaps out of her skin as though she's been stung.

She looks at the display, but it doesn't say DAD. It says NUMBER WITHHELD, and immediately she knows something is wrong.

She takes the call before the third ring.

'Hello?'

'Rebecca Case?'

A woman's voice comes down the phone at her. It's not friendly.

'Yes. What do you want?'

Her voice is weak, already failing.

'John Case's daughter?'

'Yes. What do you want? Is something wrong?'

'I'm afraid so. I'm calling from the police station. I'm afraid there's been an . . . incident.'

Just tell me, thinks Rebecca. She can tell the woman is stringing this out. She's enjoying it.

'What kind of incident?'

'Your father won't be coming home tonight.'

Rebecca holds her breath, waiting for the worst, but when she doesn't speak, the voice is forced to go on.

'He's in trouble. He hit someone.'

Rebecca doesn't really hear after that, because all she can think is, he's not dead. I thought she was going to tell me he's dead.

She doesn't really hear the rest of the phone call, and hangs up.

From nowhere she begins to cry, quietly at first, then louder and louder, until she's screaming into a cushion to drown the sound.

When she calms down, with quiet and awful anger, a dreadful compulsion comes over her.

She knows she will go mad if she does not get her father's heart back.

Right now.

1798, 12m, 16d.

Lord, have I not followed your path for all my miserable days? Have I not been a faithful servant to your mission? I confess that I have strayed. Once or twice. Once or twice, but has not my aim been true in the greater number of my days?

Why then do you turn against me?

Why turn my fellow man against me?

I grow afeared.

For I returned home this evening early, and found that Martha is not here. I have waited all evening, and though she knows to be here to cook my supper, and to warm my slippers, she is not come yet.

And if she does not come again, it can only mean one thing.

We are undone.

R ebecca moves through the crowding air like a ghost.

She carries a bag over her shoulder. It looks both empty and heavy at the same time.

It's nearly nine o'clock, but it's still amazing how hot the day has been, how humid and thick the night will be.

It's been this way all summer; the water shortages, the hose pipe bans, the cracked earth and the parched and scorched grass. The countryside is dying of thirst, everything is brown and covered with dust and sand. Ash trees in Long Lane have become so dry that whole branches have simply cracked from the trunk and fallen onto the road.

Rebecca is used to it now, but it has been unearthly, other-wordly, seemingly invincible, and eternal. But all things change, and if she had her mind on more than one thing, she might have noticed the first flashes, far, far out to sea, somewhere over the Dutch coastline.

She doesn't.

Instead, she remembers the way to the Hall.

She's only been a few times, with Ferelith, but it's not

so hard to find, even in the failing light.

She makes her way past the church, not even bothering to wonder any more at its strangeness, and climbs over the broken-down wall to the Hall.

Twisting through the stillness of the woods, dry leaves and twigs snapping underfoot, she picks up the right path.

She gazes into the dark, but can see nothing.

She stands quietly for a time, ears straining for the slightest sound. Again, nothing.

She moves on towards the Hall, and makes her way to the side, to the window they used before. As she does so, she notices a flash of light, from somewhere behind her.

Nothing, she tells herself.

But she's wrong, and as she makes it to the window, something suddenly taps her on the back. She jumps, turns, but there's no one there.

She can smell something though. The air has changed. From nowhere, it suddenly feels cold and fresh, and a sharp wind strikes her.

Something taps her head now, and she puts her hand up. It's wet.

It takes a few more taps for her to realise it's raining. It's raining fat, heavy raindrops, slow at first, but with every passing second, more and more slap into her face and body.

She turns to her work.

She marvels at herself as she smoothly and calmly takes the crowbar from her bag and levers the boards aside as though she's a professional thief.

She shoves the bag ahead of her into the pantry, and climbs through after it. She flicks her dad's powerful torch alight, and sets off into the heart of darkness once more.

She's totally unaware that she's been seen.

What Must Be Done

I can only describe it like this.

It was like a spell.

A magic spell, a witch's spell. I had worked all summer to get what I wanted and just when I thought I had lost the chance of it, it came to me, and walked into my arms, without me even trying.

She came to *me*.

I can't tell you if up to then I had been playing games. Or something more than that. But it seemed to me later, that after the storm broke, the storm which the whole summer had been waiting for, that everything changed.

I was not controlling things any more, things were controlling me.

Moving through the silent Hall, Rebecca becomes aware of two sounds only. Her feet on the old boards, and the sound of increasingly heavy rain outside.

A strange calm has entered her, as if she has detached herself from her body, and is a mere observer. So it's really very soon that she finds herself at the door to the Candle Room.

Once inside, Rebecca feels the calm disappear, blown to nothing like a candle in a storm.

Her thoughts turn, of course, to the hours she spent in the chair, and her cheeks flush with shame at the things she said, the things she thought.

She tries to push those memories away, tries to focus on the single beam of the torch, and what it finds. She swings the light across the room, and immediately she sees something shocking.

She almost screams.

She plays the torchlight onto the centre of the room, to the chair. Except it's not there any more. Shining the light now to the sides of the room, she finds the chair against a wall.

There is no explanation for this; it's as if a poltergeist has been at work.

She drags the light back to the centre of the room, and this time she sees what she did not before, something that at once explains and confuses the situation.

There is a hole in the floor. Beside it lie some serious tools. A crowbar, and a mallet.

Where the chair once stood is a gaping hole, surrounded by splintered boards.

Rebecca approaches the hole cautiously.

Then, from nowhere, footsteps sound behind her.

A voice she knows well.

'So. You came back.'

She turns, and there's Ferelith, looking, in the glare of Rebecca's torchlight, like a demon.

The girls stare at each other, and in the silence Rebecca is again aware of the sound of a storm outside, so loud that it's even penetrating into this, the very centre of the Hall. There's one other thing she can hear, and that's the beating of her heart, pounding like a fist.

She looks as Ferelith slides into the room, towards the hole.

Ferelith crouches down on all fours like a cat, and shines her lamp down.

Rebecca wonders if she hates her.

She can't decide.

Ferelith strokes the floor with her fingertips.

Because she can't think what else to do, Rebecca moves over and crouches on the floor next to her. She wonders if she's terrified, but even if she is, she's not going to let Ferelith know that. Not any more.

'Look at that,' Ferelith says, waving her lamp. She speaks as if nothing ever happened between them, here in this very room. No horror, no fighting, no crying.

Rebecca looks into the hole, and now she sees.

232

'Oh God,' she says. 'You were right.'

She can see down easily enough, down the tunnel that leads away from the chair, sloping at an angle of more than thirty degrees, a long high and wide tunnel, leading away into the darkness.

As far as they can see, it has no end.

Rebecca shudders.

'What do you think used to happen in here?' she asks. 'Really?'

'What do you mean, really?'

'Well, they didn't actually summon angels, did they? Or devils.'

Though even as she says it she wonders why she hesitated over the word. Devils. It's only a word, after all.

'Didn't they?'

'No, they didn't. Because devils don't exist. And neither do angels.'

'Don't they? Are you sure about that? I mean, you might be right, but are you absolutely sure?'

Rebecca shakes her head.

'I'm not wrong. They don't exist. Any more than fairies, or UFOs, or the yeti, or the afterlife, for that matter.'

'I thought you believed in God before? Have you changed your mind?'

Rebecca is surprised to hear her own answer.

'Yes,' she says. 'I think I have.'

'When did that happen, then?'

It happened in this very room, Rebecca thinks. You changed me. But I'm not going to tell you that.

'Dunno,' she says. 'So what about you? You never did give me a proper answer.'

'To what?'

'There you go again. You can't ever be straight, can you? Why don't you see if you can give me a straightforward answer. An honest answer, what you actually think. You know what I'm asking. Do you believe in God?'

'Oh, that,' Ferelith says. She's quiet, but eventually she answers. 'Yes, I do.'

'No buts? No maybes? No smart answers?'

'No. I do believe in God.'

'And?'

'There is no and.'

'Yes there is,' says Rebecca. 'I can feel it.'

Ferelith sighs. She leans a long way into the hole and directs her lamplight as far as she can make it go.

She pulls her head out again, and looks at Rebecca.

'I do believe in God, but given the evidence of His nature, I have to conclude that it's not a happy thing. It's not a good thing. If God exists, then God is empty. Just like me.'

'I don't understand,' Rebecca says.

'No,' says Ferelith. 'Nor do I. But that's how it is.

God is empty, His world is a painful mess, with so little beauty and order and very, very much hate and horror. But I believe He exists. And the Devil. And Heaven, and Hell. And angels. And an afterlife. Even an afterlife.'

'Why? Why do you believe that?'

'Because I have seen a white crow.'

'I don't understand.'

'Yes, you do. I told you once. About the white crow. If there's one white crow in the world, it means that not all crows are black. It means that someone, sometime, somewhere crossed to the other side, but they came back. They came back to tell us. To tell me.'

Rebecca's throat is dry.

'To tell you? To tell you?'

'Yes,' says Ferelith. 'To tell me.'

'What did they tell you? Who told you?' Rebecca whispers, her eyes wide.

Ferelith turns away from Rebecca and stares at the floor.

'It was a few days after my mother died. I was at home, lying on my bed.'

'Your old home? Before the Rectory?'

'The Rectory is my home. It always has been. Those losers who live there do so with my permission. They pay me rent. And it was there it happened. I was lying on my bed, in my room.

'It was a few days after my mother killed herself. And

then without any warning, she walked into the room, and straight up to the bed. She looked down at me, and she said this: Look behind the mirror. That's all. Look behind the mirror.

'And then she turned and left, and went, and I never saw her again.'

Rebecca is silent, but she has to ask, though she knows she needs to do it gently. 'Are you sure you didn't dream that? Or imagine it, or something. You must have been very upset, and . . .'

'No. I didn't dream it. Because I didn't know what she meant. I got up and I went and looked behind every mirror in the house. There was nothing behind any of them, and then I came to her room. My parents had separate bedrooms, and I came to her room, and she had this big mirror propped up on the mantelpiece over the fire, leaning against the wall.

'And behind it I found the book of poems she'd given to me on my eighth birthday. The poems all about me. I hadn't seen it in years. And when I read it again, I saw she'd stuck some extra pages in the back, and written a whole bunch more. New poems. New poems about me. So that's how I know I didn't dream it, because she told me where to find it.'

'That's . . .' Rebecca begins, but she stops, because there's no one word for the strange, creepy, sad, beautiful happening that Ferelith describes. Instead she

236

asks, 'What did the new poems say?'

Ferelith shakes her head. Then she answers in a small voice.

'They weren't nice.'

She stops, and Rebecca is speechless. She wonders what on earth Ferelith means by 'They weren't nice'. Something about the way she said it fills Rebecca with an unnameable terror. She can't conceive of how a mother would do bad things to her own daughter.

She suddenly feels very empty herself, and sad.

'So,' says Ferelith eventually. 'Why did you come back? Did life get too dull without me?'

Rebecca takes her time before she answers.

Something shifts inside her, something in the way she feels about this strange girl she's come to know well, too well perhaps. Yes, she's strange, but she's not a freak, and suddenly she regrets calling her that in those texts. What she is, Rebecca realises, is lost.

Unbearably, irredeemably, terribly lost. Rebecca sees that she herself has always been loved, by one person at least. Ferelith hasn't. That's what sets her apart.

Ferelith is still waiting for her answer.

'So?' she says. 'Why did you come back? Because you couldn't live without me?'

'Far from it,' she lies. 'But I lost something, and I think I lost it here. In this room.'

'What did you lose?'

Rebecca suddenly realises there is more than one answer to that question, but rather than say that what she really lost was a friend, she decides to tell Ferelith nothing at all.

Kneel and Disconnect

I'd found something amazing.

I'd opened up a hole in the floor as wide as I was tall.

I'd spent a few days working on the chair, and then the floor. The boards that the chair was bolted to turned out not to be part of the floor: they were on some kind of hinged trap, that would have let the whole section angle and sink into the floor, and then, the most amazing thing: two rails, running away, like a miniature train track, down a long sloping tunnel.

I unbolted the chair and released the trap door for the first time just a couple of hours before Rebecca came and found it. I'd gone home to get something to drink, something to eat before I went on, and came back to find her, as if she was waiting for me.

We knelt over the hole and stared.

It was incredible.

Now, with Rebecca beside me, I knew it was a sign to explore, but she didn't seem interested, and was searching around the floor of the Candle Room with her torch.

I climbed into the hole.

'Hey!' I called to her. 'Coming?'

She ignored me, so I called again.

'I could do with some help.'

Still she scanned the floor with her torch.

I looked up under the section of floor on which the chair stood.

'It's on wheels,' I told her. 'This whole section is on wheels. They're set over the rails. The chair must have run down here. Backwards.'

Now Rebecca came over to me.

The skin on my neck began to itch and tingle.

'Come on,' I said.

Rebecca froze.

'What? Where? Down there?'

'Of course down here. You can't tell me you don't want to know where it goes?'

Rebecca didn't answer.

'There could be treasure,' I said, as if I was a kid in a story book.

'Or there could be something . . .'

'Something what?'

'Horrible. Bad,' she said. 'I don't know. Evil.'

'But I thought you just told me there's no such thing as evil.'

'There isn't,' she said.

'So come on, then.'

And she did, leaving her torch on the floor beside the hole, but leaving it lit, so we could see the mouth to the tunnel all the time.

She climbed down into the hole after me, and little by little, we edged our way into the shaft. It was quite easy, because the rails on which the chair ran were set into sleepers, which we braced our feet against to climb down.

It was like walking down a ladder on a hillside, and the roof of the tunnel was high enough to take the chair with ease.

The shaft was well built, and had been bricked and shored up with cross beams every few feet. It was old, the bricks were the tiny old-fashioned sort you see on ancient houses, and the wooden beams were rough, though strong.

I went first, and Rebecca came behind, holding the lamp, which cast strange elongated shadows of us both up and down the tunnel. I had limbs as long as a spider's, I felt like an alien being investigating the archaeology of another world, another dimension.

And then, we reached the end.

We had gone maybe thirty metres down the tunnel, and it came to an end, but clearly not its original end, because there was a wall of bricks right across the tunnel, but the rails ran on underneath.

We got right up to the wall, and saw it was a very different thing from the tunnel walls. It had been hastily put together, from bricks and stones of different types and sizes, but it was strong.

It was very strong, and though we tried to kick at it for a while, lying on our backs, it wasn't going anywhere.

'What do you think?' Rebecca asked.

'What do you mean?'

'What's it for? Why did they put this here? What's on the other side?'

'Well,' I said, 'I think that's the right question. I mean, I think that if we knew what was on the other side, we'd know why it was bricked up like this.'

Rebecca nodded.

'So now what do we do?'

'Go back up for the tools, come down again and try and break it down. Yes?'

'Okay.'

'You wait here,' I said. 'I'll go and get it.'

'No,' she said.

'What?'

'That would mean taking the lamp. We'll both go. Together. Right?'

So I knew she hadn't forgiven me entirely.

'Fair enough,' I said, so we started to make our way back up the tunnel, rung by rung, sleeper by sleeper.

I can't remember exactly when the lamp went out, but it did so without warning.

242

As it did, Rebecca moaned quietly.

'No,' she said. Just that. No more.

'It's all right,' I said. 'We'll find our way out.'

And I knew we would.

We began to climb towards the mouth of the hole, where Rebecca's torch still shone.

'Don't go too far ahead,' Rebecca said, and we moved on, but after a while I couldn't sense her behind me any more.

I stopped, and then I heard she was crying.

'What's wrong?' I asked. 'What is it? We have to keep going.'

She sniffed a bit more.

'I was thinking. About my dad. He's locked up in a prison cell. Tonight. Like he's a prisoner, when he's actually a policeman. A good man. He hasn't done anything wrong. Anybody could hit some idiot reporter, you know?'

'Yeah,' I agreed. 'I think you're right.'

'He's alone and I'm stuck down this stupid tunnel and if we never get out . . .'

'We're going to get out,' I told her.

'But anyway, it's just been so rubbish between us, but I don't know what to do any more, or what to say, or how to be.'

I thought for a moment. I was getting really cold and stiff, and I wanted to move, but I could tell I needed to get Rebecca out of her blackness first.

'You said he hasn't done anything wrong,' I said. 'Yes?'

'Yes.'

'But what about the whole thing. Do you think he did wrong. About that girl?'

Rebecca didn't say anything, but sat in the dark in silence, thinking about what I'd said, I guess.

She didn't move, or speak. She just sat there.

I fished in my pocket and in the gloom, I found her hand, pushing the heart-shaped pendant into it.

'I found it. I knew it was yours. I thought you might want it back.'

From the way her breath caught in her mouth, like she was holding back the tears, trying not to sob, I knew I was right.

She did want her father's heart back, after all.

Across the Breeze

And then, before either of us could say anything at all, the world began to fall apart.

It started with a low vibration, a groan and a rumble and a crack.

Heedless of the dark, we scrambled up the tunnel. I hit my head on the floor as we got to the top, but by then I didn't care.

The Hall was shaking.

Bits of the ceiling started to fall on us, and though they were probably just tiny bits of plaster, it was terrifying.

I groped my way to the door of the Candle Room.

'Don't leave me!' Rebecca shrieked, grasping for my hand.

Hand in hand, we staggered into the hall, and I tried to get us towards the kitchens and the pantry, but as we came out into the entrance hall again, we stopped, because it was raining. Indoors.

Then the world shook again. A terrible roar of failing wood and gusting wind tore through the room, and I guessed that the roof had given way, or been ripped off.

'It's the storm!' I yelled stupidly over the noise.

Rebecca couldn't hear me, even though I was standing right by her.

'The storm!'

More rain fell on us from somewhere way above our heads, and with it some bit of the building giving way deafened us.

We both screamed, and I think that was the first time I was really afraid for our lives.

Still blind, I pawed my way along the corridor that led back to the kitchens. Panicking, we pulled each other out of the pantry window, kicking the boards completely off this time, since there was no need for subterfuge any more.

We stumbled out into the storm.

Hell had arrived and ripped into the coast. The storm that had started in Holland had torn across the channel and thrown itself at Winterfold.

Trees were threshing madly, bending low to the ground in places, and every now and again there was a tremendous tearing noise as one of them was uprooted, though even this noise was drowned in the maelstrom of the wind and rain battering us from all sides.

'Oh God! What shall we do?' Rebecca screamed. To run through the woods now seemed like suicide, and behind us the Hall was making its own threats to collapse completely.

'The footbridge! It's stone. We can hide underneath till the worst is over.'

So we took our lives in our hands, and ran towards the

bridge, throwing ourselves under its protective arch and gasping for breath.

And there we lay, listening to the destruction all around us, as the lightning flashed across the woods like a horror film, and the thunder banged, right over our heads.

But if we thought that was the worst of it, we were wrong, because from nowhere, our small bit of the world literally fell apart.

Dawn breaks, and casts a weak light on the remains of Winterfold Hall.

In a gully underneath the old stone footbridge, two girls lie against each other, exhaustion having overcome their fear and the cold and the wet, so that they sleep a troubled sleep in each other's arms.

The storm has destroyed the woods, the Hall is a ruin, the roof gone, the floors collapsed; it looks like a pile of matchwood crushed by a giant's foot.

Rebecca stirs, and shivers. She opens her eyes, and sits up, and then she sees something that makes her scream.

She's not looking at the Hall, but in the opposite direction.

Ferelith sits up too, rubbing her head. Blood flows onto her hand, and she realises that something must have cut her head during their escape from the Hall.

Fresh blood stains her soaked T-shirt, but she doesn't care.

Neither does she scream, but she swears silently under her breath as she sees what Rebecca has seen.

When they hid under the footbridge, the cliff edge,

at the bottom of the path, was twenty metres away. At least.

Now, the edge of the cliff is within a stone's throw of where they lie cowering.

'It's collapsed. My God!' Ferelith says, standing up.

The whole landscape has changed. The woods are decimated, unrecognisable; they can hear the crash of the waves beneath the new cliff edge easily now, so close they can smell the sea.

Rebecca stands up too.

'We could just have been . . .'

She stops, but Ferelith nods.

'And no one would have known. We wouldn't have known it either. Here one minute. Then . . .'

The two girls say no more, and without a word, start walking towards the new edge of the cliff.

Somehow, coming so close to death, they are heedless of danger, and stand at the very brink.

The whole coastline has changed for a few hundred metres.

'Jesus!' cries Ferelith. 'Look! The church!'

But there's no church to be seen. It's gone, almost entirely, swallowed into the sea in a single night. All that remains, now visible through the shredded woodland, is the boundary wall and a few graves, lucky enough to be further inland than most.

'Come on,' says Ferelith.

There's nothing else to do. The way the cliff has collapsed has cut them off, leaving them on a kind of peninsula. There are two paths off and both appear equally dangerous. But there's a path down to the beach, that looks just possible to scramble down. From there they can walk along the shore, and home. If the tide's out.

There's nothing to be scared of.

So they start to climb down, and then Rebecca sees something in the side of the cliff.

'What's that?' she asks. 'A grave?'

'Yes, I think so,' says Ferelith. 'No. No, it's too big. It's way too big.'

They scrabble sideways along the fallen earth and stones, and get close enough to see that halfway up the new cliff face is a gaping hole. A chamber, hidden from view for only-God-knows how long, now exposed to the bright still morning.

It gapes dreadfully like a wound in the side of a horse, and there's stuff hanging from it; bits of wood; long boxes. The hole is partly closed on one side, a smashed mouth, but nevertheless they can see it goes some way inside the cliff.

'What is it?' Rebecca asks, over the noise of the waves below. The sea churns, a thick brown and angry mess, eating away already at the newly fallen soil that the storm has presented to it.

'I don't know. But you know something . . .'

'What?'

'Our tunnel. Our tunnel pointed out to sea. Our tunnel pointed to the cliff.' She stops, and lifts her hand, jabs a finger towards the chamber. 'Right about there . . .'

Bones of You

It didn't take much doing.

It didn't need any discussion.

We both knew we were going to get inside that chamber.

The hole was in a section of the face that had fallen off, sheer and almost vertical, but we soon realised that it wouldn't really be so hard to scramble over to the cave mouth.

From there, the beach was a long way down. Somehow, though we both knew that to slip, to miss a hand- or foothold, would be to fall and die, we were not afraid. It was just something that had to be done.

I turned to Rebecca.

'You first?'

She shook her head.

'You first.'

'I was afraid you'd say that.'

But actually, it wasn't so hard. Going across wasn't hard at all. I moved myself bit by bit, and though my arms ached and complained, very quickly my feet found the edge of the cave mouth, and I staggered in.

'Come on! I'm there!' I called, and by the time Rebecca's

face appeared in the chamber's entrance, I had already seen everything.

I saw the chamber.

It was large.

I saw the rails coming from the tunnel, entering the small room, coming to rest against a huge iron stop, into which was mounted a massive blade, at neck height, I guessed. It was rusty, almost completely eaten away, and yet it still looked terrifying. Absolutely lethal.

I saw boxes. Saw that they were roughly made coffins. Some lay spilled on the floor. I saw the skeletons inside.

I saw that they had no heads. Not one of them.

And I saw the niches in the wall, and in those niches, I saw seven skulls. Above each one was a label, written in a spidery hand, and so faded that I couldn't really read the writing. I think I made out a name; it might have been Mason.

And I saw the eighth body, the eighth skeleton, and this one still had its skull, lying a little way up in the tunnel, as if heading for the outside.

We were silent.

I was filled with the horror of it all.

It was time to go.

I don't know what it was that made me do it. Maybe I wasn't thinking straight. I don't know, I just don't know.

Not really. I'd been playing games, all summer. At least I think I had. But when I decided, as we agreed to climb back out, to send that girl down to the rocks, I knew I wasn't playing games any more.

The girl had to go, that was all I thought. I'd had enough of her, and she had to go, and find out for both of us what lies on the other side.

And do you know, she didn't find it hard to die.

In fact, it seemed to be really, really easy.

1798, 12m, 24d.

The morrow is the day of our Lord's coming on earth, yet I will pay Him no heed, nor His idle father.

It has been long long days since I last wrote in this book. And I will not write in this book for much longer, indeed I write now for the last time, perhaps.

When I wrote last, I heard the knock upon my door. What do sounds convey to us? How can it be that from the mere sound of that knock alone, I knew trouble had come? For it was not the knock of the kindly passer-by, or the concerned parishioner, or the troubled soul. It was a hammering of the enemy.

My heart fought to betray me, as I made my way down the stairs, and to the front door.

As I opened the door, among the rabble and taggle there, in the thick of the angry crowd, I saw Martha.

She saw me, and looked away, and so I knew I was correct. At her side stood a small boy, whose slim figure reminded me that I had thought a ghost troubled us at the Hall, when in truth, in truth . . .

What?

What is *truth*, now?

I have killed it.

They called for me.

I stood in the door and they called for me, and though they had brought iron and steel with which to hurt me, yet they did not dare, for I am of the cloth, and they still have the fear of God living in them, that I myself set there!

But oh!

They did call and wail and were ready to ignore the bounds of God and tear me limb from limb, and then I saw my only possible path ahead of me.

– Come, Children! I cried.

This was mine.

My moment. My skill. I knew my worth, for I have stood in the pulpit a thousand times and I have made these same cries to the world. These same lies.

I know how to speak lies and to make them sound like the truth.

– Come, Children! Hear me!

And now they heard. They listened to my call, and they swallowed my bitter lies, as if they were sweet honey.

– We are all betrayed, I cried. We are all betrayed by the evil in our midst. A foreign devil! The foreign doctor! He is at work among us and we have all been duped by his wrongnesses. We must go now. We must take him! Now! Now!

And in their eager hate, the stupid sheep took all my words as the gospel of the Lord, and they did rush, streaming with terrible vengeance through the village and towards the Hall, shouting and cursing and waving their sharp irons above their heads.

All of them went, save one.

Martha.

She stood alone, after the others had gone, and she stared at me.

And then she spake not, but she did shake her head at me, and made the shapes of words with her lips.

So, now, did I understand the shapes of her lips, and her words were these!

– You are the Devil. *You* are the Devil.

And I shuddered and I fell on the floor, for now at last I saw that these were the very same words that our seventh, Mason, had mouthed to me, before his eyes had closed for the last time in his severed head.

– You are the Devil. You are the Devil.

Tomorrow is the Lord's day, the day He came upon us, and by chance it is the day that the doctor will be bricked up alive, in the chamber he built, with the remains of his doings around him.

Our doings.

My work here is done.

I leave tomorrow, for who knows where, but one thing I do know, is that I will take not God with me, for He is empty, and I shall go alone.

Resurrection

The earth quakes, the graves burst open, the dead arise and stream on in endless procession. The trumpets of the apocalypse ring out.

There is no judgment,
   no sinners,
   no just men,
   no great
   and no small;
   there is no punishment
   and no reward.
   A feeling of overwhelming love fills us with bliss.

We know, and are.
   And we know with all certainty.
   God does not exist.

When I Am Dead And Worshipped

No, it's not so very hard to die.

Fall from the cave mouth. Dead girl on the rocks below.

Easy.

Of course, when they found Rebecca, she was half mad, having been left in that chamber with eight skeletons, for hours on end, too hysterical to move, too scared to run the risk of the climb again.

It was her father who found her. He'd got himself released, because as soon as Rebecca was reported missing, all hell broke loose.

It didn't take them long to work out who she was with, but then in the storm, it took forever to find her, till her father, walking on the beach with one of the search parties, heard her cry from the cave mouth.

I saw them, reunited.

I know that Rebecca told her father what he needed to hear. That she believed in him. That she loved him still.

I know, from the way they held each other, that she did. And as she did, I could see just from the way he stood that something was healing, and that he'd found the strength to go on, to face whatever was coming for him.

And the dead girl?

The girl lying broken on the rocks below?

Well, I knew she had to go.

Ferelith had to go, and it only took the blink of an eye to step from the cave mouth. To hold my head high, and to give in to that urge, and just let go.

I was sick of her misery and her miserable life, and in a way, it was what I'd been waiting for. Rebecca and I had uncovered the truth behind the legend of the Hall, and it had taken its toll on us both.

Rebecca appeared to the rescuers to be so exhausted and upset that she'd become delusional. She told her father that I'd been with her in the chamber the whole time, talking to her, soothing her, telling her to never stop loving her father again, when they knew that she'd seen me leave the chamber first, and fall, to my end.

They tried to convince her of that, but she wouldn't believe them. She would never believe them. She would always believe that after I fell, I came back.

As I had promised.

It was what my whole life was for, I see that now. And dying was not such a bad thing, because it was worth it.

For I am the crow.
 The white crow.

WHITE CROW
AUTHOR'S NOTE

Why *White Crow*?

There were three main inspirations for this story.

The first is the place – Winterfold is very loosely based on the ancient settlement of Dunwich on the Suffolk coast, which, like Winterfold, was once a thriving medieval town, now just a quiet curiosity of an English seaside village.

Second, was the incredible, but true, account of a scientist, Dr Beaurieux, who genuinely tried to communicate with the still warm head of a guillotine victim. He concluded that consciousness persists for up to thirty seconds after beheading. Here's a chilling excerpt from his notes:

I waited for several seconds. The spasmodic movements ceased ... It was then that I called in a strong, sharp voice: "Languille!" I saw the eyelids slowly lift up, without any spasmodic contractions ... but with an even movement, quite distinct and normal, such as happens in everyday life, with people awakened or torn from their thoughts.

Next Languille's eyes very definitely fixed themselves on mine and the pupils focused themselves. I was dealing with

undeniably living eyes which were looking at me. After several
seconds, the eyelids closed again…

And in case you're wondering when this happened, the guillotined man was not a victim from the days of the French Revolution; Dr Beaurieux conducted his experiment on an executed prisoner in June 1905.

Finally, the White Crow itself refers to a quote by William James, the American psychologist and philosopher, (and brother of the novelist Henry James), who became fascinated with the possibility of the afterlife, around the height of the Spiritualist movement at the end of the 19th century.

"If you wish to upset the law that all crows are black, you mustn't seek to show that no crows are; it is enough if you prove one single crow to be white."

With these elements in place, I then used Rebecca and Ferelith's stories to weave them together, and bring Winterfold to life. And death.

This is my eleventh novel for Orion, and looking back I can safely say that each and every one would not have been half the book it became without the graceful and precise skills of my editor, and publisher, Fiona Kennedy. Thanks be to you.

Marcus Sedgwick
Hadstock
January 2010